King of Realms

Britt Asher

To Nate,
who inspired me to be a creative geek

Contents

'

Chapter 1

The Theft

V arric had to steal the relic or his mom would die.

That's what he kept telling himself as he dangled upside down from a tree branch over a castle walkway full of guards—guards who would gladly throw him in a dungeon for the rest of his life—or worse—if they caught him. It didn't matter that he was barely twelve years old. Stealing from the king was usually frowned upon, regardless of the thief's age. How did he always end up in these situations?

Peering through a cluster of leaves, Varric scoped out the castle tower where they kept the relic. He'd hoped the Centennial Tournament would lure away some of the guards, but security in the area was as thorough as ever. Three guards were exiting the tower after performing one of their routine searches. It was time for Varric to make his move. He'd only have a short period of time to get in, get his prize, and get out before the next search.

As soon as the guards stepped outside and locked the door behind them, Varric teleported into the tower. He landed on his back with the entire tree branch squishing him to the floor. He really needed to learn how to *not* teleport junk with him. Rolling the branch aside, he stood, dusted himself off, and looked around.

He'd gotten a peek inside the tower during his earlier scouting missions, but he hadn't had a chance to investigate the rest of the building. Luckily, he didn't see any traps or sneaky guards. He climbed a spiral staircase to a circular room at the top of the tower. A crystal light on the ceiling shone over his prize: the magic relic of Iloria. It sat on a pedestal lined with Orbeel traps. Anyone dumb enough to touch it would set off all sorts of defenses and alarms.

Varric paced around the pedestal. He'd expected the relic to look more interesting. It was round and flat like a plate, had two handles underneath it, and was made of green metal. Three Orbeels were embedded in its side. Like most Orbeels, they looked like pearls, but these ones shimmered with various pale colors. They gave the relic its magical ability that let it show anything that existed within the realms. It was one of the most powerful items in existence, and it was the only thing left that could save Varric's mom.

His father's former advisor, Jonavad, had sent him to steal it, insisting it would help her. Varric had thought they'd use it to look for a way to heal her, but Jonavad said the relic's magic was useless and that he'd use it for something else. Varric didn't understand, but he trusted Jonavad. Still, he figured he'd try using the relic's magic anyway, just in case. He owed it to his mom. After all, it was his fault she was dying.

Something crashed outside, and a chorus of screams pierced the walls of the tower. Varric only had time to frown. The wall across from him exploded, sending a barrage of high-speed bricks flying in his direction. He dove for the floor and shielded his head with his arms as chunks of stone pounded him. He'd definitely have some nice bruises later. His ears rang over the sound of blaring alarms.

Sunlight flooded the room through a newly formed hole in the wall, and some sort of creepy bug beast now sat on the pedestal. It was almost as big as Varric, and it looked like an ugly ant with four leathery bat wings and a hooked tail. It also had two arms with pincer claws, and those pincer claws seized the relic.

"Hey! That's mine!" Varric hopped to his feet and drew his dagger.

He thought the beast might try to escape. Nope. It unleashed a high-pitched screech and lunged at his face. He yelped in surprise and stabbed at it, but it flicked aside his arm with its tail and sent his dagger skittering across the floor. He ducked under another tail swipe, only for the beast to tackle him from behind, knocking them both to the floor. Something sharp pressed between Varric's shoulder blades, and searing pain flooded across his skin. He jerked to the side and punched the bug in one of its nasty, squishy eyeballs. When the beast recoiled, Varric rolled and kicked it with both feet. It went flying, bobbled on its wings, and zipped out of the tower through the hole, taking the relic with it.

"Stop! I need that!" Varric snatched his dagger off the floor and ran to the hole—and froze.

Several shining white portals appeared in the sky, and dozens of bug beasts poured out of them. Some of the beasts swarmed the forest around the castle and city, but most attacked the sprawling field of grass where the Centennial Tournament was being held. Hundreds of screaming people fled the field.

Anxious flutters filled Varric's stomach. Memories crowded his mind of when his realm collapsed and people screamed for help—for his help—and he couldn't save them. His fingers tightened around his dagger, and he glanced at the chunk of rainbow crystal that formed its blade. It could stop the beasts, but revealing his magic to others would put him at risk. Besides, the Tournament contestants seemed to have the situation under control. Fireballs, rocks, and water flew all over the field as the contestants fought back against the bugs. Some of the strongest magic users in the realms had gathered to compete in the Tournament for a chance to claim one of the relic's three uses. Now they rallied together to protect the realm. They were tough and would probably be fine. Still, Varric couldn't bring himself to run away, not when he knew he could help.

"Stop right there, thief!"

Varric jumped in surprise, whirling around to find five guards pouring out of the stairwell. The screams and alarms had drowned out their footsteps.

"Return the relic," a guard shouted.

Varric looked around for the bug beast with the relic before awkwardly realizing they were looking at him.

"I didn't steal it," he exclaimed. "It was a beast! It—"

"Save it for the king." All five guards closed in on him. "You're under arrest."

Varric teleported from the tower before any of the guards got close. He landed on the Tournament field and jabbed his dagger into the nearest bug beast, making the beast disappear in a flash. The blade of Valkaris had one specialty: with a touch, it sent beasts into the beast realm and trapped them there forever. Varric teleported around the field, poking every beast he found. He got lost in a blur of leathery wings and movement. The whistle of wind and the shrieks of beasts drowned out the screaming.

No, the screaming had stopped. Varric halted and found the bug beasts fleeing into portals until none remained—not even the one with the relic. His stomach sank. Now what was he going to do to help his mom? Jonavad was going to be furious.

Light flashed in the corner of Varric's eye. He turned toward it, only for a bolt of magic to hit him in the chest. A chilling wave of energy washed over him and made his magic wither, blocking his ability to teleport. Varric staggered from the hit and flinched as he saw a small army of Ilorian guards closing in on him.

"Hold it right there, Interloper," shouted one of the guards.

"You're under arrest for the theft of Iloria's relic," hollered another.

Varric turned on his heel to run, but one of the guards tackled him while a dozen others surrounded him. Most wielded spears, but three men carried magic blasters powered by gray Orbeels: temporary magic blockers. One of the guards ripped his dagger out of his hand while two others yanked him to his feet and closed a shackle around his wrist. It had a gray Orbeel embedded in the metal. Varric's throat pinched in terror. The blaster bolts would block his magic for a little while, but the shackle would block his magic for as long as he wore it. He jerked from side to side to break free from the guards, but their grips didn't budge. They dragged him toward the castle on the edge of the forest. Dread clenched his lungs and suffocated him.

"Not so tough without your magic, are you?" a guard scoffed, shoving Varric forward.

"Tough?" Irritation mingled with Varric's increasing terror. "You mean when I fought off those beasts for you?" That earned him another shove.

People on the street stared at him with open hostility. No one seemed to care that he'd tried to help against the beasts. Instead, they muttered about him—the vile Interloper that broke into their realm to cause all sorts of chaos.

"You're welcome for saving you," he grumbled, but they just glared harder.

The guards hauled him into the castle, their footsteps echoing in the stone hallways. Waterfalls poured from the ceilings, grass sprouted through the floors, and trees grew through the walls. Plant life flourished everywhere. It was a neat place, but he would have appreciated it more if it wasn't the last place he'd ever see. Interlopers didn't get slapped on the wrist. No, they got death sentences. He was going to die in a castle full of flowers.

Varric's heart hammered faster with every corner they turned. They dragged him through a huge pair of doors into the throne room and down a long green carpet, where they shoved him to the floor before the throne. He sat on his hands and knees and kept his head down so his hood hid his face.

The king sat on his throne, his fingers thrumming the armrest. He had the typical Ilorian dark skin, hair, and eyes. He wore a fancy green tunic with lots of silvery gold decorations. A royal assembly of nobles in fancy clothes gathered on either side of the green carpet. Guards with shields and spears lined the walls. A girl stood among the guards closest to the throne. Most of the guards were middle-aged men, but she couldn't have been much older than Varric. She looked out of place, but she definitely wore the same green tunic and leather armor as the rest of the guards. Her threaded hair hung in a low ponytail over her right shoulder. The bottom quarter of her hair was dyed gold.

"Well, Interloper, what do you have to say for yourself?" the king asked. "Where is my relic?"

"I didn't steal it," Varric murmured. One of the guards hit him in the side with the butt of a spear. Gritting his teeth, he raised his voice. "I didn't steal it. A beast broke in and took it."

"A beast? And how did they get here?" the king asked. "I have no doubt your interloping had something to do with those portals."

Varric made the mistake of making eye contact with the king and immediately dropped his head. The guy had murder written all over his face.

"I didn't bring them here," Varric said.

"Forgive me if I don't believe you."

"You're forgiven," Varric muttered, which earned him another jab with the spear.

A chorus of voices erupted from the hallway. Several guards scrambled in ahead of a buff guy wearing dark, ragged clothes. His sleeves had been torn at the shoulders, revealing thick arms. He had tousled dark hair and short, scruffy facial hair. Judging by his tan skin and strange clothes, Varric assumed he was there for the Tournament. Even as guards threatened him with spears, he grinned and sipped out of a wooden mug, sauntering in like he owned the place.

"So, this here's the Interloper that caused all the fuss, eh?" he asked. He eyed Varric and took another sip. "Kinda small, aren't they? You guys arresting babies?"

"Who is this man?" the king asked.

"An accomplished contestant in the Tournament, Father," said the girl with gold-dyed hair. "He was rapidly advancing."

Varric stared at her, bewildered. If she hadn't just called the king *Father*, he never would have guessed she was the princess.

"Why is he here? Go back to your games." The king waved him away and returned his sharp glare to Varric. "Enough of this. Show me the vile creature who dares to steal from the king of Iloria."

Two guards grabbed Varric and tore back his hood. The room filled with the sounds of startled gasps, and everyone's eyes went wide when they saw him.

"A child? That's impossible!" a nobleman exclaimed.

The buff guy's cup fell and clattered to the floor, spilling his drink. "H-he really is a baby, isn't he?" he said, his voice wavering. He shook his head and forced a smile, and after a moment, it looked more natural. "How old are you, kid? Eight? Nine?"

"Twelve," Varric snapped. He hated when people underestimated his age. It wasn't his fault he was short.

"A twelve-year-old Interloper?" a noblewoman said.

"It's not possible."

"Unheard of."

"Silence," the king shouted, and the room went still and quiet. "Tell me, boy. How did a child your age acquire the powers of an Interloper?"

"How does anyone acquire their magic?" Varric asked. "I was born with them."

"The powers of an Interloper never appear in children. It's impossible." The king's eyes narrowed. "You'd do well not to lie to me."

"I'm not lying. And I didn't steal the relic."

"We saw him in the tower, Your Majesty," said a guard. "He was the only one in there when the relic was stolen."

"A beast broke through the tower and stole it," Varric interjected. "Didn't you see that big hole? I can teleport. Why would I blow a hole in the wall?"

"Why would you be in the tower in the first place?" the princess asked.

Oops. Varric lowered his head. Dark strands of his messy hair fell over his face, hopefully hiding his burning cheeks.

"I was going to steal it," he admitted pathetically. He did feel bad about it, after all.

Murmuring erupted throughout the room, and everyone glared at Varric. To them, he was one of the worst things in the realms. Interlopers could freely hop from realm to realm. No one could stop them. As long as an Interloper had seen a place, they could teleport there. Interlopers throughout history assassinated monarchs, robbed people of their riches, and caused all sorts of mayhem. They'd become the villains of childhood fairytales.

"Enough." The king rose from his seat. "You broke into my castle and attempted to steal our realm's treasure. Furthermore, you're an Interloper who now has permanent access to my throne room. We of Iloria have no tolerance for your kind here. Interloper, I sentence you to death."

Chapter 2

An Explosive Situation

E ven though Varric hadn't eaten in a few days, he still almost threw up. The room broke out in a chorus of chatter, even as the king called for silence. Varric barely heard any of it. Instead, he heard the king's death sentence repeated over and over in his head. His ears rang as his heart thumped faster and faster. He'd messed up big time. Who would help his mom? Who would look after his sisters? Jonavad was there to take care of them, but he didn't have magic. They needed Varric.

"Hold up, there!" The buff guy stepped forward, his arms crossed and his brow furrowed. Anger clouded his eyes. "You can't be serious. This kid is literally a baby and you're executing him?"

"Why is this man still here?" the king snapped, gesturing angrily in the man's direction.

The guards clamored around the buff guy, but he was big, bulky, and couldn't be moved. They apparently didn't poke Tournament participants with their spears. The guards buzzing around him didn't faze him in the slightest. The tallest of the guards only reached his nose, and he looked right over their heads.

"He's a little kid. Can't you show him mercy?" the man continued.

"I'm not a little kid," Varric muttered, though no one heard him over the yammering in the room. What a dumb thing to say, anyway. He'd been sentenced to death, and he was worried someone thought he was little? Yikes. Priority check.

"He would be the youngest execution in the history of Iloria," the princess said, wrapping her arms around herself. "Father, it's unheard of. Is this truly a mark we want on our family?"

"And what other mark shall we have, Daughter?" the king asked, and nothing in the question sounded like he wanted an answer.

She stiffened at his tone and bowed her head. "Forgive me, Father. I spoke out of place."

"What else can be done?" the king's voice boomed throughout the room. "Does anyone have any alternative punishment for a creature as vile as this Interloper?"

A chorus of voices throughout the room answered the king.

"Shackle him and lock him up!"

"Execute him!"

Waves of shivers ran up Varric's spine at the hatred in their voices and in their eyes as they looked at him. He swallowed bile, but it came right back.

"I have an idea," said a new voice from the open doorway.

All voices silenced and all eyes drifted to a man who walked in with great pomp and authority. It was the guard who'd taken Varric's dagger. Like most of the natives in Iloria, he had a dark complexion. He wore his hair in long braids separated in rows at his scalp. His beard was trimmed short and framed his mouth.

"What say you, Wark?" asked the king.

The man called Wark approached the throne, scrutinizing Varric as he passed and looking at him the way someone might look at a mangy street dog. He said, "The guards finished analyzing the tower. They discovered traces of a beast within the barrier around the relic. With Pellios's help, they should be able to use those traces to locate the beast." Wark's eyes rose to the king. "I propose you send this Interloper to retrieve the relic on our behalf."

"Just let him go?" the king asked.

"Have you forgotten, Your Majesty?" Wark offered a slight bow, the beads in his braided hair clattering over his shoulders. "We received that new device from Pellios that I have been most interested in testing."

The king's eyebrows went up, and realization dawned in his eyes. A slight smile curled his lips. He sank back into his seat in a most comfortable position. "Very well. Bring it."

"I thought you might say that." Wark pulled a silver item from a pouch on his belt and grabbed Varric's arm.

"Let me go." Varric pulled against the man, but the grip on his upper arm tightened to the point of discomfort.

Wark twisted Varric's arm and yanked it out from under his cloak, setting the silver item on him. It fully wrapped around his wrist and clicked shut. Varric shook his arm, but the bizarre cuff bracelet barely budged. A single red Orbeel decorated the top of the cuff. Like most Orbeels, it had a faint glow.

Varric held it up. "What is this?"

"An explosive device from Pellios," the king said.

Varric's heart leaped into his throat. He stretched out his arm and kept the bracelet away from his body.

"An explosive," the buff guy exclaimed.

The king shot him a glare before directing his hostility toward the guards. Everyone heard the unspoken words: *why is he still here*? Even then, no one tried to remove him.

The buff guy heatedly added in protest, "He's a little kid!"

"I'm not a little kid," Varric murmured with zero enthusiasm. He could hardly breathe, and his heart hammered so hard it throbbed in his ears. The bracelet looked so shiny and harmless.

"I've provided you a great mercy," the king said to Varric. "By the rule of law in our realm, Interlopers must die. However, I'm giving you the chance to redeem yourself. You will retrieve the stolen relic and return it to Iloria. Then I will remove the explosive bracelet and consider your release."

"I don't know anything about the beast that stole the dumb thing," Varric said, heat rushing to his cheeks. His head was swimming, and he could barely concentrate. "How am I supposed to find it? This is impossible!"

"That's why I'm giving you this." Wark drew a small, clear Orbeel out of his belt pouch and set it in Varric's hand. "This Orbeel has the information we collected from the magic barrier that shielded the relic. You'll take it to Pellios and use it to track the location of the beast throughout the realms."

"I'll give you two weeks to complete the task." The king leaned back in his seat. "If after two weeks you haven't returned with the relic, I'll detonate the explosive. I can control it from any realm and any distance, so don't bother trying to run. And I'm the only one who can remove it. If you try to tamper with the Orbeel, it detonates automatically."

"How am I supposed to search all the realms and find this beast in just two weeks? It'll take me a while to even get help in Pellios." Varric squeezed the clear Orbeel and drew it to his chest. It was his lifeline. If he lost it and failed at his mission, he was dead.

"Then you better get moving." Wark grabbed Varric's other arm and removed the shackle that had sealed his magic. He felt his strength return to him in a rush—not that teleporting would help him much now, traveling to places he'd never been.

"Can I at least have my dagger?" Varric asked.

"I'll hold on to it for you," Wark said. "Until you return with our relic, of course. Consider it a pledge of your loyalty."

Varric gritted his teeth and struggled to regulate his breathing. Fear for his life mingled with frustration. They didn't care if he succeeded, did they? If he died, it wouldn't bother them. They were going to execute him anyway. And if he died and didn't come back, they would be able to keep Valkaris. But it was his dad's dagger. It belonged to his family. He'd be back for it, no matter what.

"Fine. I'll get your dumb relic." Varric huffed at them, squaring his shoulders.

"And how can we be certain the boy won't use the relic prior to returning it to us?" asked a young woman who stepped out of a crowd of attendants. She wore a golden gown, lots of jewelry, and had her hair in tight curls. She looked especially angry—at everyone and everything. "The royal family only has three opportunities to use it every century. We can't waste those uses on an untrustworthy street urchin."

"True . . ." The king stroked his chin hair.

"I'll go with him." The princess stepped forward, her face fierce and her head held high.

The king raised an eyebrow. "You? Why?"

"I can ensure he returns the relic without using its magic," the princess said, sounding defeated at the disapproval in the king's tone. "Besides, the relic is far too important to Iloria to leave its fate in the hands of a stranger. For the sake of the realm, I'll ensure its return."

The king sighed, his face drawn. Quiet muttering resumed among the people. The nobles and guards seemed more impressed by the princess's dedication than her father did.

"Do as you want," the king muttered.

"I'm going, too," said the buff guy.

"Who *are* you?" the king asked in exasperation.

"Argo, from the realm of Yerevir," the man said with a striking grin.

"And why would you want to endanger yourself to return the relic?" the king asked.

"I wouldn't feel right about letting kids go alone," Argo said. "I can protect them."

"I don't need protecting." Varric fluffed his cloak to make himself look a little bigger. No one listened to him.

"Besides," Argo continued with resolve, "I came to Iloria to win a right to use the relic's magic. I can't use it if it's stolen, can I? How about I help retrieve the relic and you let me use it when I return?"

"How can I be sure of your worth?" the king asked. "I've hired common mercenaries before and found them lacking."

"I'm not a common mercenary," Argo crossed his arms. "I'm a Tournament participant. And I was on my way to winning the Tournament before the beasts decided to ruin my fun. Go check the standings. I was about three fights out from victory."

The king didn't appear impressed until Wark whispered into his ear. Then his eyebrows went up.

"Very well. Tales of your battle prowess precede you. I permit you to escort them. Know that if any harm comes to the relic, you will have the full wrath of Iloria upon you," the king said.

"Sounds pleasant. But don't worry. I'll get the job done."

"Fine," the king said. His sharp gaze locked on Varric. "Succeed and earn your freedom. Fail at your peril. Now be gone from my sight."

Several guards ushered Varric down the carpet and shoved him out of the throne room. The princess and Argo only had time to step outside before the doors were slammed shut behind them.

Chapter 3

The Shifter and the Bonder

"**G**ive that to me before you lose it." The princess snatched the clear Orbeel out of Varric's hand while he was inspecting it.

They'd exited the castle and wandered a ways down the street. Varric had investigated the cuff explosive on his arm, which appeared to be a solid piece of metal that didn't open. He decided not to play with it and risk blowing himself up, turning his attention to the clear Orbeel instead.

"They gave it to me," Varric snapped. He swiped at it, but she dodged and shoved him away with her shoulder. She was bigger than him and stronger than she looked. He tottered off balance and gave up trying to retrieve it. "What is it, anyway?"

"An Orbeel. They're beads made of different types of compressed magic."

"I know that. What does it do?"

"Clear Orbeels contain information that you can read and process from certain tech devices." The princess stuffed the Orbeel in a leather pouch on her belt. "This Orbeel collected the information of the beast that broke into the tower, which will make it easier for us to track it."

Varric didn't completely understand, but he figured he'd learn what he needed to know when they reached Pellios.

"Where are we going, exactly?" Argo asked, his fingers laced behind his head, casual as could be. "The transport station is the other direction."

"Pellios could take weeks to process this information for us," the princess said. "I'm taking us somewhere where we can figure things out a little faster. We're going to visit someone who used to help at the castle until she had a falling out with my father. Her name is Bernadea. She lives on the far eastern reaches of the realm."

"You're sure this is faster?" Varric asked, eyeing the explosive on his wrist. He liked faster.

"Yes. I don't want to be out here with you for any longer than necessary. I will return the relic to Iloria, and I will return it quickly."

Varric huffed at her retort but left it alone. At least she knew where they were going so they didn't waste time wandering around. They walked along the street in silence.

Several streetlamps had been broken during the beast attack, leaving much of Iloria City in darkness. The tall trees and thick canopy blocked most of the sunlight. Only portable lamps and lights from open windows shone onto the street.

Several market stalls had been overturned during the attack, their food, clothes, and trinkets scattered on the ground. Two suspension bridges dangled from the trees, leaving people stranded in their homes built in the branches. Guards brought ladders to help them down. Thankfully, most of Iloria's buildings were made of sturdy stone blocks mingled with thick trees, so the beasts hadn't damaged them.

At one point, the princess stopped to buy some supplies for their journey, including a water skin for Varric. Then they resumed their march. The princess walked at a slight distance from Varric, which he didn't mind. Argo remained close to them, but slightly behind, like a creepy guard. Varric glanced at him over his shoulder. The man was staring intently at him and made no attempt to hide it. Instead, he flashed a huge grin at Varric. Definitely weird. He looked like a thug or mercenary, like someone who could wrestle a bear—and win.

Varric sighed as they passed through the city gate, which consisted of two huge wooden doors that always stayed open. The doors were pointless because the city had no walls. The forest got fuller for a while, with tons of underbrush and creeping vines, and then dwindled. The thick canopy thinned and gave way to sunlight. A few wooden houses existed on the edge of the forest. Most people that far out wore simple tunics and worked in huge vegetable fields. The stone road ended, replaced by a gravel trail that was overrun by grass and weeds. It led to a sunlit field of grass and wildflowers not unlike the Tournament field. The road went on forever with no end in sight.

"How far away is Bernadea?" Varric asked.

"About a day's walk from the city. We'll reach it late, so we'll have to set up camp and contact her in the morning." The princess scowled at Varric like the thought of camping with him was horrendous. Then she sighed. "My name is Setia. What's your name?"

Varric ignored her question and kicked a pebble on the rough trail.

"Look, I'm not really excited about being here, either," Setia grumbled. "But we're traveling together for now. We may as well call each other by name. It'll make things a lot easier and a lot less awkward."

"You didn't have to come."

"I have my reasons." Setia avoided his eye contact.

"What reasons?"

"Tell me your reasons for trying to steal my family's relic and I'll tell you my reasons for coming here."

Varric rolled his eyes and stared straight ahead, ignoring her.

Even if he wanted to, he couldn't share his reasons. Reasons led to questions he couldn't answer. If he told them he wanted to steal the relic because his mom was dying, they'd ask what happened to her. Then he'd have to explain that his home realm imploded eight years ago and crushed her, leaving her mind and body withering away into nothingness. Then they'd wonder how a realm could implode. He'd have to explain how his dad had tried to open a forbidden pair of magical doors and set off a defense mechanism that destroyed the realm.

Jonavad had warned him never to talk about those things. If people knew the truth about Varric's father, their family would be in danger. His mom would be blamed for her husband's horrific actions. Varric and his baby sisters would be cursed for sharing the tainted blood of a man who killed countless people. Their family would be hated, feared, and condemned.

No, Varric wouldn't risk that. His mom and sisters were safe in hiding with Jonavad, and Varric planned to keep it that way. He couldn't trust anyone—besides Jonavad, at least. Varric couldn't even trust himself. After all, he'd had the magic to save his mom, but he'd failed to do it. She was dying because of him. He couldn't tell anyone that, either. Teleporting and being a thief were bad enough. He didn't want people hating him because he'd ruined his mom's life.

"Since you won't tell me your name, I'll have to make up my own names to call you," Setia said after they'd walked in silence for a while. She wouldn't even look at him. "Thief? Scamp? Maybe I should just call you Interloper—"

"My name is Varric," he snapped, glaring at her.

"That wasn't so hard, was it?" Setia returned his glare before shifting her attention to the buff guy clomping along behind them. "And you're Argo. You're a Bonder, correct?"

"I am."

"Bonder?" Varric eyed the guy with a fair level of respect. "That means you can summon beasts to fight for you, yeah? What sort of beasts have you bonded with? What can you summon? Something big and scary?"

"Cute little puffballs, actually. Maybe I'll show you sometime," Argo said with his usual grin. "Meanwhile, Princess Setia is an exceptional Shifter, or so I've heard. How come you didn't play in the Tournament?"

"I didn't need to win the right to use the relic. The relic can be used three times, and two of those times are reserved for my family." Setia brushed off her tunic and armor for no good reason. Then she adjusted the bracers on her wrists for no good reason. "But yes, I'm a Shifter."

"What beasts did you steal powers from?" Varric asked. "What sort of magic can you use?"

"Perhaps I'll show you sometime," she replied, keeping her eyes straight ahead, basically ignoring him.

Varric couldn't help feeling disappointed. Sure, he could teleport through realms, but Bonders and Shifters were way more interesting. Bonders could form connections with beasts that allowed them to summon the beasts from any realm at any time. Most Bonders could only summon little beasts. If Argo had made it far in the Tournament, he'd probably bonded with more interesting and dangerous beasts. Meanwhile, Shifters only had to touch a beast to copy their magic. The crystals lit throughout Iloria City were illuminated by Shifters who used the magic of Brightlings, beasts that always glowed. The powers of Bonders and Shifters seemed so much more exciting than his own magic. Most people didn't hate Bonders and Shifters, either.

As they walked, Setia held out her hand. A silver spear appeared in her grasp in a flash of light.

Varric jumped away from her. "Where did that come from?"

"This." Setia held up her wrist and showed a green Orbeel on her leather bracer. "It's an Orbeel that stores physical objects."

Varric couldn't help but stare in wonder at it. "How do you make it go in and come out?"

"I just think it and it happens."

"Can I think it and make it happen?"

"No." Setia's eyes narrowed in distrust. "The Orbeel attaches to an individual user. Only I can use this one now that I'm connected to it. Only I can move the spear in or out."

"What if you die?" Varric asked, wondering if the spear would get stuck in the Orbeel forever.

"What if I don't?" Setia's face darkened. Huffing, she stormed ahead on the path.

Varric sighed. Girls were complicated.

They continued on for a while in silence. Setia twirled her spear in intricate patterns. Sometimes she slid forward and thrust the point of the spear like she was stabbing something. Varric didn't know much about weapons, but she looked skilled. Rather than stare at her, which might be a little awkward, he looked up. Over a dozen winged creatures swooped in the sky high over the field. Their feathered white wings looked enormous, but their bodies looked like nothing more than a black speck.

"Winglings," Setia said, as if reading his mind. "They love flying in windy places."

"It isn't windy," Varric pointed out. He hadn't noticed anything more than a slight breeze.

"It probably is up there," Argo said. "It gets pretty windy the higher you go."

"Yerevir is rather mountainous, isn't it?" Setia asked.

"Sure is."

"Aside from what I've studied, I don't know much about your realm." As she spoke, Setia continued her spear drills, twisting and stabbing like she was dancing and fighting at the same time. "I've heard your queen is well respected."

"I'm fond of her," Argo said with a light chuckle. "She's easy on the eyes, too."

Varric blushed for Argo. The guy seemed to say whatever came to his mind. Setia stopped long enough to roll her eyes and then resumed stabbing.

"What did you do in Yerevir?" she asked. "When you weren't traveling to other realms to compete for a chance to use their relics, that is."

"Oh, you know . . . traveling here and there."

"You were a thug, weren't you?" Varric asked. "You beat people up for a living. Sword for hire. You took people out. Not very stealthily, but you didn't have to be. You just crushed them so there was no one left to talk about it."

"That can't be true," Setia muttered, shaking her head.

Argo shrugged, grinning. "He might have the right idea."

"Then what's your true purpose for being here?" Setia asked, taking the whole situation way more seriously than

Varric expected. He bit his lower lip to hide a smile as she got worked up. "Do you intend to take the relic? Are you a thief?"

"If I am, I'm not a very good one since I signed up for the Tournament in the first place," Argo said. When Setia sharpened her glare on him, he raised both hands in innocent surrender. "Okay, I'll admit I'm here right now for a different reason." Hooking his thumbs on his belt, he asked Varric, "Say I help you get the relic and earn your freedom from Iloria, how about you help me pull a prank on someone?"

"A prank?" Setia halted, her eyes wide in disbelief.

"What? Why me?" Varric asked.

"Your interloping skills would be mighty useful for what I'm planning."

"Is it illegal?" Varric may have been caught stealing, and he did steal food to survive, but he didn't actually *want* to be a criminal.

"Well . . ." Argo scrunched his face and looked everywhere but in Varric's eyes.

"I can't listen to this. You can't be serious." Setia slammed the butt of her spear to the ground with a thud. Even as Varric and Argo walked past her, she didn't budge.

"No one would get hurt. And the kid wouldn't get in trouble. It's not that it's illegal, really . . ."

"Very illegal, when you put it like that," Setia snapped. "Have you no honor?"

"No."

Varric snickered, but he shook his head. "I don't really like breaking the law."

"You were stealing from my family," Setia growled.

"Out of necessity. You wouldn't understand." Varric caught a glimpse of the nasty scowl she gave him and diverted his attention back to Argo. "I don't really like it."

"No one gets hurt. I promise." Argo slashed a finger over his heart to make an *X*. "You won't even be blamed. It's not bad like you're thinking. And in the end, we'll all have a good laugh about it. Probably." When Varric shifted uncomfortably, he added, "Consider it, at least? I'll help you get free and prove my worth. You'll see I'm not such a bad guy."

Setia snorted. They ignored her.

"I guess I can think about it," Varric said, his cheeks still warm. No one had ever really shown any interest in his powers, besides hating him for them. It felt weird that someone would want him to use his magic to play a prank on someone. It sounded like something a friend would ask him to do.

"I'm going to pretend I didn't hear any of this. Shame on both of you." Setia marched past them and stormed up the trail. She threw in a few angry spear thrusts, too. Maybe she was imagining giving them a few unfriendly pokes right in their backsides.

The thought made Varric smile. He couldn't help but notice Argo grinning, too.

Chapter 4

Bernadea the Hermit

"Are we still in Iloria?" Varric asked, eyeing the building at the far edge of the realm.

The house was spectacular in a way that made Varric's eyes refuse to blink. It was two stories tall and looked like several miniature houses crammed into one building, with sections sticking out at odd angles and windows facing every direction. Despite the bizarre shape, the house had tidy white boards and neat gray trim. A black metal fence surrounded the crisp green yard.

Most of the wild woods had been left behind, and only a copse of thin, twisty trees provided any cover to Bernadea's house. Beyond the house was the shining white wall that marked the edge of the realm. The ground and sky simply stopped.

"Even though she's from Iloria, Bernadea doesn't really get along with us," Setia said, scratching her cheek. "You'll see.

She's a bit eccentric. But she's one of the most brilliant minds among the realms."

"How did she build such a weird house?" Varric asked.

"With magic, probably." Argo led them to the gate.

It was barred shut. A shiny square panel with an embedded blue Orbeel was mounted on the metal gate. The panel had a button on the bottom. Varric reached to push it, but Setia slapped his hand and pushed it herself. The square panel flashed, and an image appeared. It looked like a room cluttered with furniture and junk.

"Who's there?" asked a female voice out of the panel.

"What is this?" Varric leaned forward to get a closer look. "Where is that voice coming from?"

"Who is this?" the woman's voice asked.

"Princess Setia Fay'orin, here on an errand from the king. Please permit entrance to me and my companions."

Some scraping noises erupted from the panel, and then it flashed and turned back into a shiny square. Varric pressed his hand on it. Nothing happened. He looked at it from all sides and saw nothing else interesting about it.

"It's tech from Pellios," Setia explained. "They use Orbeels for a lot of unique things. This one lets you see and communicate with someone from a distant location. Bernadea has a matching screen and Orbeel inside her house. She could see and hear us."

"How come I haven't seen anything like that in other places in Iloria?" Varric asked. He jumped away as the metal gate screeched open on its own.

Setia led the way up a brick walkway edged on both sides by flowers and bushes. "Iloria generally doesn't like Orbeels. We don't use them unless it serves a necessary purpose for our people. We prefer things to be more natural."

A metal mouse crawled through the grass and snipped a dead branch off a shrub and ate it. It rolled around and munched through everything dead, leaving a pristine yard and garden behind.

"On the other hand, Bernadea loves Orbeels," Setia said, eyeing the mouse gardener. "It's part of the reason she secludes herself."

"Looks like it saves her a lot of work," Argo commented.

"We in Iloria prefer to get our hands dirty and do the work ourselves." Setia climbed onto the white porch. "It isn't merely about looks but about the effort we put in to produce results. Some of us find satisfaction in a hard day's work."

"Can't say I disagree," Argo said. "Yerevir isn't big into Orbeels, either. Not as much as somewhere like Pellios, at least."

When they got close, the front doors hissed and slid apart on their own, vanishing into the walls on either side. Varric stared in shock at the doorway as Setia and Argo entered. Neither seemed afraid the doors would slam shut on them. He scurried after them and jumped over the threshold. After he'd passed, the doors lazily slid shut.

"Bernadea?" Setia called out.

Varric turned from the sliding doors to the interior of the house. Beyond the entrance hall, the house was full of all sorts of junk. Furniture and piles of metal and wood were stacked to the ceiling. Shelves were buried under metal trinkets with Orbeels attached. Tech devices, he assumed. He wanted to play with them to see what they did.

Setia led them into the main area, which was one huge room. Something thumped behind them, making Varric jump. A rainbow-tinted crystal sat on a pedestal against the wall. Something bounced back and forth in the crystal, making lots of noise.

"What is that?" Varric asked.

The thing inside the crystal stilled. It had a human torso and a long fish tail instead of legs. Curly fins and webbing all over its body made it look wispy and feathery. The creature had long hair, pointed ears, and jewels all over its body. Every inch of it was blue. It glared at Varric, clawed at the crystal with its webbed hands, and resumed thrashing against the crystal walls.

"Is that a Waveling?" Setia wondered, leaning for a closer look.

"A Waveling you'd do well to avoid, Princess," said a woman's voice.

A strange clacking sound arose from the other side of the house. A woman erupted out of another room riding a bouncing stick made mostly of metal. Every time the stick hit the ground, it scrunched low and then sprang up again, clacking on the tile floor whenever it landed. The woman bounced across the room to them, then bounced in place in front of them. She scrutinized them through enormous round glasses with various lenses. Her dark skin starkly contrasted her white hair, which was curled into two wild buns on either side of her head. Fairly short and round, she wore a full-body suit that fit her snuggly.

"That Waveling is the one that tried to drown Iloria," the woman said, all while bouncing.

"You still have it?" Setia asked. "That was over a year ago. I thought you intended to send it back to the beast realm?"

"I went through the trouble of catching it. May as well use it to advance my research for a while. I've learned quite a bit about the beasts and their magic, thanks to this little one."

"It looks like a fish." Varric stepped over to the crystal to get a closer look, but the Waveling bared its fangs and redoubled its efforts at flinging its body against the crystal walls. Varric moved so that Argo was between him and the crystal.

"I haven't seen it this ornery in a while. It doesn't like being bothered. Nor do I," said the woman, glowering at them.

"Forgive our intrusion, Bernadea. It's good to see you again." Setia offered a warm smile. It actually made her sort of cute. Much better than her scowly face.

"Hmm." Bernadea scrutinized each of them through her glasses. When her eyes found Argo, she muttered, "Not bad," but when she reached Varric, her gaze locked. "A little mangy, this one. Doesn't smell very good, either."

"I smell fine," Varric grumbled, heat stinging his cheeks. He pouted and sniffed his cloak. It had been a while since he'd washed. He hadn't had a real bath in a long time, but he dipped in rivers and lakes when he could.

"What do you want, Princess?" Bernadea asked, not sounding pleased.

"I need you to examine the information on this Orbeel. We're looking for an escaped thief who stole something important from my family." Setia held out the clear Orbeel.

"Ah, yes. The relic of Iloria was stolen. I heard about that." Bernadea kept bouncing as she snatched the Orbeel from Setia. Then she bounced across the room.

Varric, Setia, and Argo glanced at each other and followed her. She led them to an assortment of metal boxes with flat panels similar to the one outside.

"How did you hear about it already?" Varric asked. "We came straight from the castle after it happened."

"I have my ways. Word gets around fast when you deal in information." Bernadea bounced to one of the box devices and plopped the Orbeel into a slot on top. Letters and pictures flashed across the device, none of which made sense to Varric.

"Why are you bouncing?" he asked, earning an elbow from Setia. She glared at him, but he ignored her.

Bernadea scrutinized them and then scrunched her face to one side, all while bouncing. "A lady my age needs to maintain a thorough exercise routine to keep fit and active. Can't slack and take it easy. Once you stop, you never get up again." She shot them each a nasty glare. "Not that you youngsters have any idea what that's like. You take everything for granted, don't you? How old are you?"

"Twelve," Varric replied.

"Fifteen," Setia said.

"Thirty-five." Argo grinned, his muscular arms crossed—arms so strong he could probably lift Bernadea and her bouncing stick in one hand and launch them to the ceiling. "But I hear ya. I get a little creaky if I sit around too long. Still, I prefer to enjoy my exercise. What's the point of doing it if it's not fun?"

"Who said this isn't fun?" Bernadea scoffed as she bounced.

"I think it looks fun. Can I try?" Varric took a step forward, but Setia elbowed him again. He grumbled, "Stop doing that."

"Stop bothering her," she muttered through gritted teeth.

"Don't worry. You're all bothering me equally," Bernadea said without a hint of remorse. "Anyway, you can use my hopping stilts later. Right now, I have your information. Lucky for you, the beast you're looking for is a known troublemaker." Even as she bounced, she managed to push buttons on a pad on the table. Each button had a letter on it, and the pad itself was connected by a cord to the box device. "This particular beast tried to break into Pellios only a month ago. It fled before getting caught, but they captured its information when it broke into their facility."

"What did it try to steal?" Setia asked.

"It seemed to be scouting various facilities without targeting any one thing. They've had several beasts doing that recently, though they're not sure how they're getting into the realm." Bernadea tapped away at her buttons. "It's a Wasteling, an uncommon beast known to dwell only in the realm of Clobalt. The Wasteling returned to Clobalt after it departed from Iloria."

"You can tell all that just from that Orbeel?" Varric stared at the panel and the clear Orbeel attached to the top.

"The Orbeel gave me the signature of the beast that stole the relic. I tapped into Pellios's info-base to locate it. Pellios keeps track of all the realms as much as possible and monitors who comes and goes."

"They can do that?" Varric took a step backward, his chest tightening. "Can they track Interlopers?"

"If they've scanned an Interloper, they can track them." Bernadea leaned forward on her so-called hopping stilts, inching closer to Varric. "That's an oddly specific question, isn't it? Why do you ask?"

"No reason."

"What do they do with all that tracking information?" Argo asked.

"Not much," Bernadea said. "Pellios collects information, but they don't infringe on the rights of other realms. Their work helps us in instances like this, though." She flipped down the extra lenses of her glasses, making her eyes look huge on her face. She inched a little closer to Varric. "That's a curious bracelet you're wearing."

"So you're certain the Wasteling returned to Clobalt? That's where it's at now?" Setia shuffled to the side, partially blocking Varric from Bernadea's view. Bernadea's sharp eyes shot in her direction, her lips sinking into a frown that made her cheeks sag.

"Seems so," said the older lady. She removed the spare lenses and bounced back to the tech device, poking buttons. "It returned to Clobalt yesterday and hasn't since departed."

"Good. Then we have our next destination." Setia placed a hand on her chest and bowed toward Bernadea. "Thank you for your help. We'll be on our way now."

"Hmm," Bernadea said, bouncing in place.

Setia led the way to the door. Varric and Argo followed. The clacking of Bernadea's stilts ceased, followed by a loud clatter. Varric turned to find Bernadea charging toward him. She grabbed his wrist and yanked it out from under his cloak, revealing the explosive bracelet.

"Be careful with that!" Varric yanked his arm back and cradled the bracelet. The last thing he needed was some crazy old lady blowing it up on accident.

"That's definitely Pellios tech. What does it do?" she asked.

Varric glanced at Setia, who shook her head.

Bernadea harrumphed and plopped her fists on her wide hips. "I did a favor for you, Princess. Give me the scoop."

Setia sighed and rubbed her brow. "It's an explosive that my father can detonate. Varric is technically a prisoner of Iloria until he retrieves the relic."

"Prisoner? Why? You're so little." Bernadea waved her hand from the top of her head to the space over Varric's head, showing their height difference. She was a little taller than him. Varric waved her hand away.

"He tried to steal the relic," Setia said.

"Oh! Did he now?" Bernadea cackled, showing slightly uneven teeth. "Bold little urchin, aren't you? Varric's your name?" Varric nodded, and Bernadea leaned closer. Her nose wrinkled, and she retreated several steps. "Needs a bath." She grabbed her hopping stilts off the ground and resumed bouncing. She turned her attention to Argo. "What's your story, muscle man? You're not from Iloria."

"Name's Argo. I'm the babysitter." He offered a two-fingered salute from his forehead. "I'm a Bonder. I fight things. Break stuff. From Yerevir."

"Send me some goat milk, would you? I could use some cheese." Bernadea waved them away with her free hand. "Now go. You've interrupted me long enough. Scoot."

Varric scurried after Setia to the self-opening door. Argo brought up the rear as they departed from the bizarre house full of bizarre things.

Chapter 5

Portals to New Places

Varric had never been to Clobalt, so he couldn't teleport there. They returned to Iloria City, where Setia arranged transportation for them at the city transport station. Few people traveled to Clobalt, so they had to wait a couple of days for the station to get permission from Clobalt first. Varric hated that they had to waste two days waiting for the realm to let them enter, but a small part of him was excited about seeing a realm where few people were allowed to go.

On the day of travel, they sat on wooden benches in the transport station and waited for a station attendant to open the portal for them. Like every other place in Iloria City, the station's architecture was a blend of stone and trees.

Argo had bought meat and veggie skewers for them from one of the few remaining Tournament vendors. Argo had already finished his, and Setia was almost done with hers. Varric only took a few bites of his before folding his leftovers into the wrapper. He didn't know how well it would preserve until later, but it never hurt to have back-up food. Even though Argo and Setia kept giving him food, he never knew when that might stop. He tucked his leftovers into his belt pouch, earning a raised eyebrow from Argo.

Since the Tournament had ended, the station bustled with people leaving Iloria. An entire wall was covered by portal stations, which were metal-framed devices powered by Orbeels that created portals to other realms. The destination realm had to have an active receiving portal station in order for them to work. Clobalt deactivated theirs when they didn't want guests—which was apparently all the time.

Varric kicked his feet, hoping the station attendant would return soon so they could be on their way. He distracted himself by picking at the explosive bracelet on his arm. He'd gotten comfortable with it at that point, because Setia had assured him it wouldn't explode unless her father detonated it.

As people shuffled by, they gave him harsh looks, some crinkling their noses and giving him a wide berth.

"Everyone keeps staring at me." Varric burrowed deeper into his cloak and pulled up his hood.

Setia leaned past Argo to look Varric up and down before slumping back in her seat. "It's because you look unkempt. And you're dressed like a thief. Why didn't you come to the castle and bathe while we were waiting?"

"I didn't want to." Varric crossed his arms.

In truth, the last place he wanted to be was at the castle where everyone hated him. Argo had gotten a room at the inn and offered to let Varric stay with him, but Varric didn't like the idea of letting his guard down near someone he didn't know. Not that he had much to steal now that his dagger was gone, but still. He'd found a comfy spot in the roots of a tree where he'd slept in peace, without the risk of being bothered or hurt by anyone.

"I should order you to bathe and change your clothes," Setia said, only sounding half joking. "You're technically part of my entourage right now. Your unkempt appearance and behavior reflect poorly on me and my family."

"All the more reason I shouldn't take a bath," Varric muttered. Setia glared at him, but Argo grinned.

"I like your attitude." Argo rubbed the top of Varric's head.

"Don't encourage him," Setia grumbled.

"Princess Setia?" An attendant wearing a leather suit hurried over. "Your portal to Clobalt is ready. They have permitted only a small window of entrance, so you should make haste."

"Understood."

The attendant led them across the station in a direction with fewer people.

"Neither of you have been to Clobalt?" Varric asked Argo and Setia.

"Never," Argo said.

"No. I've only studied it." Setia finished her meat and veggie skewer and tossed the stick into a trash bin as they passed. "Their realm exists in the sky, most of the inhabitants are Shifters, and they're highly focused on scholarly pursuits. They generally don't permit outsiders or get involved in outside affairs. Bernadea was once offered an opportunity to join their community, but she took great pleasure in snubbing them."

"Clobalt people are so crazy even Bernadea avoided them? That's not a good sign." Varric blew out a breath and shook his head. Argo chuckled, but Setia glared at them.

"Be on your best behavior," she commanded. "We're guests who could very well be thrown out."

"Yes, ma'am," Varric and Argo said in unison. They grinned at each other. Setia rolled her eyes.

The attendant led them to a portal station that wasn't in use by anyone else. It had a metal panel on the side with two Orbeels attached: one white and one clear.

As Varric contemplated why the device needed two Orbeels, Argo whispered, "The white one powers the device and the clear one tells the portal where to go."

The attendant pressed a few buttons and stepped aside. "You may proceed to Clobalt, Princess."

"Thank you for your assistance."

Setia led the way up the platform, glanced at Varric and Argo, and vanished through the portal. Varric stepped through behind her, and the energy of the portal buzzed around him. Argo came after him. On the other side of the portal, they found themselves in a room with pearl-white tile walls and floors. Nothing existed in the room besides the portal, its gold frames, four pillars made of gold, and a few high windows. A big crystal light on the ceiling illuminated the room.

A man and woman approached them, drawing Varric's full attention. They had pale skin, practically without any color, and their hair was stark white and stood straight up in wooly tufts. The hair was almost as tall as the people. Varric couldn't resist openly staring at them. Argo and Setia stared, too, so Varric didn't feel that bad.

"Princess Setia of Iloria, we greet you on behalf of our queen, Lady Aurora of Clobalt," said the man. He had a young face despite his white hair. Varric had never seen white hair on non-old people. He kept staring until Argo nudged him with his arm.

"Thank you for your hospitality, and I apologize for any inconvenience. We don't mean to impose. These are my . . ." Setia stopped when she was introducing Varric and Argo, stumbling over her words. "This is my bodyguard, Argo, and . . . then there's Varric."

Varric stared stupidly at Setia. What sort of introduction was that? She could at least lie or something. Now both people from Clobalt stared at him because of her weird introduction. Their noses wrinkled and their heads tilted up in disdain.

"He's my kid," Argo explained, patting Varric on the back. "Goes where I go. Won't cause any trouble."

The Clobalt pair seemed less disdainful but still not very pleased.

"Please keep your offspring from touching anything," said the man, scorning Argo instead of Varric. Varric appreciated Argo's efforts, but he was sick of the way these fancy, hoity-toity people treated him.

"What's up with your hair?" he asked, feigning innocence.

"Varric," Setia snapped under her breath, her eyes bulging. The pair from Clobalt looked equally appalled and bug-eyed.

"That's enough out of you, son." Argo chuckled, wrapping an arm around Varric's shoulders and squeezing not very gently.

"Forgive us," Setia said, bowing at the waist. "We know so little of Clobalt, so please forgive our surprise and misunderstandings. We will not cause trouble for you. I assure you." Out of the corner of her eye, she shot Varric a look that said, *If you cause any more trouble, I will personally end you.* She continued, "An important relic of Iloria was stolen, and our search for the item has led us to Clobalt. I would like to speak with your queen to see if she is able to aid us in our search."

"You think Clobalt played a role in this theft?" The pair from Clobalt glanced at each other, neither looking pleased.

"Not at all. Only, our current information led us to believe the culprit escaped to Clobalt. I would like to hear the queen's take on the matter."

"I fear your information is mistaken. Nevertheless, our queen has already agreed to meet with you." The man stepped forward and offered them three rings with pink Orbeels. "You will need these to safely travel our city."

Setia handed them to Varric and Argo before putting on hers. "What do they do?" she asked.

"If you should fall off the edge of our city, the ring will protect you from the harsh elements."

"Fall off?" Varric echoed. He shoved the ring onto his finger. "Do people fall off often?"

The man glared at him. "On occasion."

"Mine doesn't fit." Argo put the ring on his smallest finger. It barely went on at all.

"A pocket will suffice. It will still work," the man said, his eyebrow twitching.

"You will also need these in case you fall." The woman handed each of them a strange pack with straps to slide over their shoulders. She helped Setia dress in it to show them how to wear it. "Pull this string, and it will release a glider to slow your descent."

"What happens if we fall?" Varric asked, sliding on the pack and unraveling the string so he had easy access to it.

"We will attempt to send Shifters to retrieve you."

"And if they don't retrieve me?"

The Clobalt pair exchanged looks. Then the man said, "Do not fall."

"Come this way, Princess," the woman said.

The Clobalt pair turned in harmony and shuffled toward gold sliding doors. Their long white robes swished as they moved. The golden fringes and tassels on their clothes glittered in the light, as did the gold jewelry that decorated their necks and arms. Varric and the others fell in step behind them, but Setia pinched Varric and slapped his arm.

"Stop causing trouble," she whispered through gritted teeth. "Your life is on the line, remember? We need to succeed here or we'll never find the relic. Is that what you want? Stop making me look bad."

"I'm making him look bad, now." Varric jutted a thumb at Argo. "He adopted me."

"Behave yourself," Argo said, lightly prodding the back of Varric's head with a finger.

The Clobalt woman glanced back as she stepped through the doorway. Setia, Argo, and Varric stood straight and smiled. Varric didn't like the attitudes of the Clobalt people, but Setia was right. If he wanted to get the relic and regain his freedom, he needed to play nice with others. He still needed the relic to save his mom, too.

When they stepped outside the building, Varric, Argo, and Setia stopped. They stared at the most mesmerizing and unlikely realm anyone could have imagined.

Chapter 6

The City in the Sky

Clobalt was pristine and perfect, without a single scuff or trace of dirt, and completely artificial. White and gold buildings towered over them on different platforms that floated in the air. Some of the platforms were connected by bridges. Others had smaller platforms that floated between them. Crystals shone on the ground and on pillars throughout the city, providing light. The crystals were about Clobalt's only source of light, because the sky was dark and flecked with stars. Half the sky, at least. Closer to the horizon, the dark sky faded to light blue, like they'd floated so high that they'd passed the blue sky right into the starry heavens.

"How high are we?" Setia murmured, clasping a hand over her chest.

"Quite," said the man. "Thanks to the tech of Pellios, we have ascended above our atmosphere. No oxygen exists at these levels, and a fall from this height would tear a human body apart. Thus the ring and the glider. They provide oxygen, warmth, and protection from harm." He waved them forward across perfectly shiny tile platforms. Their footsteps clacked and echoed.

A few people meandered over bridges and platforms. They stared at Varric and the others. Varric reminded himself that the people weren't used to strangers and that it wasn't entirely his fault for drawing so much attention. Everyone wore the same fancy robes and had the same upright wooly hair.

They reached the edge of the platform, which had no rails. It opened into empty space. Varric peeked over the edge from a distance. Far below, clouds puffed up and billowed out like a blanket of snow.

"We're above the clouds!" he exclaimed.

"What's below the clouds?" Argo asked.

"Nothing," the man said curtly.

"If you fell and no one stopped you, where would you go?" Varric pressed.

"You would fall forever. Nothing exists below the clouds."

Varric, Argo, and Setia exchanged bewildered looks. As far as Varric knew, all realms originated with land and sky. Humans had built their cities from the ground up. Even the people of Clobalt must have originally built their city on something solid before it began to float.

"Come. We can make haste to the palace." The man extended his hand toward the edge of the platform. White light flashed from his palm, and clouds bubbled and formed in the open air, flattening into a wide platform. The Clobalt pair stepped onto it. Their slippers sank into the cloud like they were walking on fluffy grass.

"How did you do that?" Varric asked, mesmerized. He kept his distance, though.

"Most in Clobalt are Shifters who wield the power of Cloudlings. It allows us to manipulate clouds for whatever purpose, including solidifying them as temporary walkways." The woman gestured at the open space beside her. "Come. It is perfectly safe."

"The alternative is to take a long and meandering route to the palace." The man pointed toward distant bridges and solid platforms that wandered through the air at slow paces. "This route will be much faster."

"Never ridden on a cloud before." Argo stepped across without hesitation and dug his boot into the cloud. It fluffed up around his foot, but it didn't look like he sank far.

Setia stepped across, wobbling. Argo gripped her elbow and steadied her. Only then did Varric realize Argo wasn't wearing his glider. It was slung over his shoulder.

"You like heights, don't you?" Varric asked as he stepped across. Like Setia, he tottered. The height made him dizzy, overwhelming his senses. Argo grabbed his arm. Varric sank to his knees on the cloud to keep from falling.

"I grew up in Yerevir," Argo replied. "We're used to having our heads in the clouds."

Not Varric. He hated heights. It was one thing his magic was useless against. If he teleported while falling, he would still be falling wherever he reappeared. He would splat just as hard on the ground, regardless of where he teleported.

The cloud platform slithered through the air. Despite the movement, it didn't feel like it was moving. It glided around the city, avoiding all the other platforms and buildings and carrying them straight toward a magnificent palace with tall gold spires and doors as big as the surrounding buildings. It had a big white Orbeel on top, which looked like a giant moon shining over the city. It was stuck on a gold spire.

A few beasts floated up around them. They had cloud-like bodies, puffy tails, and tiny wings that didn't flap. The beasts had big blue eyes that searched the cloud platform with interest. When their eyes landed on the riders, they squinted in anger and abruptly turned away, descending in a freefall.

"Cloudlings," Argo said when Varric stared at them.

"They usually prefer to stay in the clouds, though sometimes they come to see what clouds we create using their magic," the man said. His brow furrowed. "I have never seen them leave so abruptly, however."

Varric watched the main parts of the city grow distant as their cloud carried them all the way around to the palace. Glancing below, all he saw in every direction were clouds—far, far away clouds, like he would fall for a long time before ever reaching them. The view became dizzying. He crabbed backward until he sat on Argo's boots. Argo wouldn't exactly be the safest person if he fell over the edge—he wasn't even wearing his safety device. Still, it felt a little safer with him anyway since he acted so confident.

Their cloud approached the platform on which the castle was built. The man and woman stepped off with ease and headed toward the castle. Argo hopped off and offered Varric and Setia a hand as they climbed onto the more stable structure. As soon as they all stepped off, the cloud dissolved.

The Clobalt pair led them across the open area ahead of the palace. Guards opened the massive palace doors by pushing their palms against shiny gold panels. The panels flashed and the doors opened on their own. The guards wore the same white and golden robes as everyone else. They also wore gold helmets that covered most of their faces but had holes in the top for their stuck-up hair.

Varric glanced up at the shining Orbeel at the top of the palace as he walked toward the open doorway. He flinched at the radiant light, stark white against the star-flecked sky. A silhouette caught his eye, and he held up his hand against the glare. A dark shape loomed on the peak of a pointed tower. Varric glimpsed bat wings and a clawed tail before the shape disappeared into the shadows and lights.

"Something wrong?" Argo asked.

Varric had stopped without realizing it. That had definitely been the same type of beast that attacked him in Iloria. Or was he imagining things? Did the bright light and shadows play a trick on his eyes, making him see what he wanted to see? He was eager to catch the beast and be free of the explosive on his wrist, after all.

"Nothing," he said, though without certainty. He didn't want to bring it up in front of the Clobalt people, but he wondered if the Wasteling lived in the palace. They'd find out soon enough when they talked to the queen.

They entered the palace and found a whole lot more of the same. Everything was clean and perfect, like people didn't live there and they'd built the buildings for decoration. They wandered down several corridors until they reached another huge pair of doors opened by a panel. A guard went in ahead of them.

"Presenting Princess Setia Fay'orin of Iloria." The guard bowed, stood straight, pivoted on his heel, and marched to the side of the room.

Setia led the way to the throne. The room was taller than any other room in the castle. One part of the ceiling was made of glass, and the giant Orbeel beamed light into the room. A golden runner paved their way to the throne platform where the queen sat. Varric tripped on the rug as he got a good look at her, and he couldn't take his eyes off her. Her perfectly white, wooly hair went all the way to the ceiling.

"Stop gawking," Argo muttered out of the corner of his lips.

"Can't," Varric admitted, feeling foolish. Argo stepped ahead of him, blocking his view of the queen. Still, Varric peeked around Argo's arm. How did they keep their hair like that?

"Greetings, Queen Aurora." Setia bowed at the waist.

"Princess Setia," the queen said unenthusiastically. Her gaze drifted past Setia, slithered over Argo, and landed on Varric, who was still partially hidden by Argo's arm. Once she found Varric, her ice-cold gaze didn't move. Leaning sideways, she said to a nearby servant, "Make note that the floors will need to be sanitized. Monitor what they touch."

She acted like she was whispering, but she didn't even try to keep her voice down. Varric was getting tired of people commenting on his appearance. It wasn't his fault he didn't have nice, clean clothes. Or a nice bath. Or all the nice things they had in their fancy palaces. He made a mental note to rub his hands all over the walls before he left. Maybe lick a few door handles, too.

"Forgive us for imposing on you, Your Majesty." Setia's voice wavered in a way Varric hadn't heard before. "Thank you for permitting us entrance into your realm."

"You understand we do not take lightly to outsiders here." Aurora's eyes hit Setia again. After her whispering to the servant, she sat up straight and didn't move. Only her eyes moved, like the rest of her body was frozen.

"Yes. All the more reason I am grateful." Setia bowed again, and she remained stooped until the queen spoke again.

"Why have you sought my counsel?"

"Recently, Iloria held our Centennial Tournament. Once per century—"

"I know about your Tournament and Iloria's relic. What concern is this of mine?"

Setia opened and closed her mouth. Her calm composure cracked, and Varric almost felt bad for her. She looked like a naughty kid trying to explain a naughty situation to an angry parent.

"The relic was stolen," she said, her voice wavering. "We had a magical barrier surrounding the relic, which collected information about the thief. The information revealed that a Wasteling stole the item. According to Pellios's info-base, the Wasteling escaped here to Clobalt."

The few guards along the walls and the few servants around the throne began murmuring among themselves. The queen didn't move, but her face rippled with anger. Her lips pressed into such a tight line that they turned completely white.

"Silence," she roared, and her voice echoed off the walls and devoured the other voices. Silence prevailed. Her hands formed claws around the arms of her seat. "Are you suggesting my realm is harboring a thief?"

"Not at all, Your Majesty." Setia took a step forward, speaking in haste. "Only that perhaps a Wasteling has escaped here without your notice—"

"Do you think us oblivious?" Aurora's voice rose, even more terrifying since everyone else had gone silent. "Do you think us lacking in security and attention to detail? Your insinuation is insulting."

"That's not . . ." Setia stumbled over the words. She sounded like she might cry.

"We mean no disrespect, Your Grace," Argo said, and the queen's eyes latched onto him like a hawk on its prey. He stood tall and spoke with authority. "We simply followed the last lead available to us and hoped you might bestow upon us some of your wisdom. If you have heard of anything, or seen anything, it would be most helpful to us. If our information was in error, we apologize for our mistake. And we regret that we have no other leads than this." At that, he threw in a stiff and formal bow.

Queen Aurora looked him over, and some of the frost melted off her features. "You have a silver tongue, bodyguard. But alas, we monitor who is permitted entrance into Clobalt. No thief has come or gone from my realm."

"You are certain there is nowhere a beast might sneak in without your knowledge?" Setia asked dismally.

"No," the queen said, turning a frigid glare on her.

"Then we'll take our leave, Your Grace," Argo said. "Forgive us for pressing the matter. We have nowhere else to turn." He bowed. Setia and Varric bowed, too.

"My attendants will escort you to the portal station." The queen's harsh exterior melted at Argo's words.

The two attendants who had met them at the portal station waited for them at the door. After bowing, Varric and the others retreated from the throne.

"Bodyguard," called the queen, making them pause. "If you seek better employment, consider visiting me here in Clobalt."

Argo offered his most winsome smile, bowed, and exited with Varric and Setia.

Chapter 7

Clobalt's Stinky Secret

F ollowing at a slight distance from the attendants, Varric and Setia leaned toward Argo.

"Thank you so much for stepping in and helping like that," Setia whispered. "She kept throwing me off balance."

"Did someone take control of your body?" Varric asked, equally as quiet. "How did you talk like that? Who are you?"

Argo chuckled and kept walking without offering any explanations. Varric was going to have to reconstruct his image of Argo. There was more to him than he realized if he could smooth-talk a queen better than Setia.

They walked down the corridors in silence. Whenever the attendants weren't looking, Varric ran his fingers over the white tiles and left behind dirty smears on the walls. Maybe he really did need a bath. After he'd mucked up a bunch of walls, Setia huffed in annoyance, grabbed his ear, and pulled him away.

Once outside, they headed toward the area where they'd disembarked from the cloud platform.

"I don't think they're telling us everything," Setia whispered.

"Neither do I. Though I'm not sure what they could be hiding." Argo glanced around, scratched his facial scruff, and then eyed Varric. "Get a good look around, kid."

"You want to sneak back in later?" Varric grinned. He liked the way Argo's brain worked.

"As long as they don't know you're an Interloper, they won't know it's us."

"I can't listen to this." Setia covered her ears and walked slightly ahead of them—so she could still hear them but pretend she couldn't.

"I see some good places," Varric confirmed. With the main source of light being above, the buildings cast lots of shadows between them.

"You can't be serious." Setia fell back in step with them, her brow furrowed and her voice stern.

"You don't have to come," Varric said. He held up his wrist with the explosive bracelet. "I need to get rid of this."

"Breaking the law is the reason you're wearing that in the first place. Crime isn't the answer."

The attendants created another cloud platform and waited for them to catch up.

"Bernadea isn't wrong," Argo said. "The Wasteling must be here, and I think the queen realizes that, too. What if Clobalt stole the relic and is trying to cover it up?"

Setia's frown relented, and she didn't argue. Varric recalled seeing the Wasteling on the palace roof. He should have mentioned it.

"Still. Shame on you," Setia muttered to Argo as he climbed onto the cloud platform with the two attendants. She didn't bother whispering. "You're an adult. You should set a good example for Varric."

"I am setting a good example." Argo helped Varric and Setia onto the platform. "Never give up, kid."

Varric grinned and Setia rolled her eyes. The platform slid across the sky, returning to the area where they'd entered Clobalt. The attendants didn't seem interested in talking to them anymore. They reached the landing platform in silence and returned through the boring city streets. Nothing had changed. Few people roamed about. It was a lonely place, now that Varric thought about it. No one seemed happy. He hadn't heard a single laugh, nor had he seen a smile on any of the people in Clobalt. It made him sad for them.

Thudding sounds arose from the glowing crystals along the edge of the platform, slowing Varric's steps. The crystal closest to him thumped so hard it almost tipped over, sending him hopping sideways in alarm. The crystal rattled and rocked, its light flashing and dimming in random intervals. Argo stepped between Varric and the crystal, but then every crystal on the street started blinking and shaking like something was trying to burst out of them.

"What's going on?" Setia asked.

The light in the nearest crystal dulled, and a faint outline took shape inside it.

"There's something inside there," Varric said.

"Brightlings," said the man. "Our Shifters focus on retaining the powers of Cloudlings, and few of us are capable of maintaining more than one power at a time. Instead, we capture Brightlings and trap them in crystals to serve as our light sources."

"They're stuck in there forever?" Varric asked, horrified.

"Of course. They are only beasts."

Varric's stomach twisted into a knot as he looked at the crystal. If he squinted, it did sort of look like a wispy butterfly. He'd only seen Brightlings from a distance. They were too pretty to be trapped in a rock forever. It wasn't right. Argo and Setia looked as appalled as he felt.

"I have never seen them act like this, though," the woman said, resuming her walk down the street. "How unusual."

The attendants moved along like trapping beasts forever in crystals wasn't horrible. Varric approached the nearest crystal, his chest aching for the prisoner inside. Beasts didn't get along with humans, but imprisoning them still felt wrong. He wished there was something he could do to help them.

A shriek pierced the air and made Varric jump backward. A dark shape swooped over the top of the nearest crystal, slamming into him and sweeping him off his feet.

"Varric!" Argo and Setia shouted, but their voices were drowned out by the thumping of wings.

Varric lost sight of his companions—and everything else, for that matter. A big Wasteling body blocked his view. The creature snatched him off the platform and swooped away with him, dragging him through the air.

"Let go," Varric snapped. He swung his fist as hard as he could and punched the bug beast right in its ugly head.

The Wasteling shrieked and recoiled from the hit, letting him go. Varric went sideways, and his heart leaped into his throat as he plummeted past Clobalt City. The dumb Wasteling had carried him over the edge of the platform!

Panic muddled Varric's mind. He desperately reached for the glider string flapping around in the wind. Just as he managed to catch it, the Wasteling crashed into him and sent him spinning, making him lose his grip. The bug beast landed on his back and seized him with all six legs, frantically beating its wings like it was trying to slow him down. It wasn't helping.

"Leave me alone," Varric pleaded, waving away the bug legs now blocking his grip of the glider string.

A gust of wind tore the Wasteling off Varric's back, but only for a moment. The beast shrieked and latched on with greater vigor, grabbing at him with its mandibles and pincer claws. One of its pincers slipped under the shoulder strap of the glider and cut straight through it. The entire safety device slid off Varric's shoulders and blew away, taking the Wasteling with it.

Varric could only stare in stunned horror as his lifeline was swept away. He was doomed. Terror clenched his throat. He hadn't actually thought anyone from Clobalt would come and rescue him, but the glider would have slowed him down so he could teleport himself to safety. His mind raced for other solutions. He could probably teleport deep underwater—that might slow him down without flattening him.

As Varric struggled to think of places with deep water, he plunged into the puffy white clouds. They closed in around him like a thick and ominous fog, making him feel a hundred times more anxious. To make matters worse, the obnoxious Wasteling swooped in again, screeching and clawing at him. They tumbled out of the white fog into a brown haze. Varric was about to smack the Wasteling again when Argo fell out of the clouds and dropkicked it in the head. The Wasteling went twirling away at high speeds.

Strong arms wrapped around Varric and slowed his freefall. The falling and spinning had made him dizzy, but now his vision started to clear. Or maybe it didn't, because he was pretty sure Argo had a pair of big, dark, feathery wings on his back. Argo adjusted his grip on Varric, sitting him on his arm and gripping his legs like a parent would carry a little kid. Varric was too flabbergasted by his fall and sudden rescue to care much that he was small enough for Argo to hold that way. Instead, he grabbed Argo's neck and held tight, because he wasn't interested in falling again. Their descent slowed, easing some of his fears.

"You have wings?" Varric asked.

Argo grinned. "Something like that." He scanned the area below them, his jovial expression faltering. "Well, well . . . looks like Clobalt was keeping something a secret after all."

Varric followed his gaze to the sprawling landscape below the clouds. Pools of bubbling black sludge interrupted patches of dark and barren ground. Dark fog erupted from the sludge and filled the air with haze. From below, the clouds were dark, but enough light filtered through that they could still tell it was daytime. Off in the distance, dead trees sprinkled the horizon in the most pitiful forest Varric had ever seen.

"Definitely looks like a place for a Wasteling, huh?" he muttered. "We should check it out."

"Agreed." Argo descended toward a spacious patch of land.

Now that he'd caught his breath and regained his senses, Varric peeked over Argo's shoulder at his wings. A bird head popped up and stared back at him with eyes like midnight, dark and full of stars. Varric yelped, the bird squawked, and Argo's wings—the bird's wings—beat frantically, bobbling them around in the air.

"Whoa, whoa! Calm down, Novi," Argo called out. "He's good. He's a friend."

Novi hissed at Varric but resumed a steady descent. It continued to stare at him, its eyes narrowed and never blinking.

"I'm starting to think you're the one aggravating all these critters, Varric," Argo commented—not entirely joking, either.

"I didn't do anything." Varric ducked out of Novi's sight.

Argo landed and set Varric on his feet. Varric scrunched his face at the strong scent of decay hanging in the air. And people thought *he* smelled bad.

"Are you hurt?" Argo asked.

"No."

"Hey!" Setia swooped out of the air with a pair of white, fluffy wings. "Are you both okay?" She landed beside them, the feathery wings folding at her back.

"You have wings, too?" Varric asked.

"One of my copied powers is that of a Wingling." Setia turned, showing off her sleek wings. Unlike Argo's, hers were a part of her. No creepy birds were peeking over her shoulder.

"Jealous," Varric said, glancing back and forth between Argo and Setia. He was glad they'd both tried to save him, but he was bummed he couldn't sprout wings and save himself. Then he stopped, realizing what Setia had said. "One of your copied powers? You have more than one?"

"I have two."

"Two!" Varric exclaimed.

"It's rare to find a Shifter who can copy more than one power at a time," Argo said, folding his arms. "That's impressive, Princess."

"Apparently. But I'm not the most surprising person here." Setia pointed at Argo's wings. "What is that?"

"Meet my girl, Novi." Argo held out his arm, and the bird perched on it.

She was so big her wings looked like Argo's wings when she attached herself to his back. She had sharp, curved talons and wispy, ethereal feathers. Most of her feathers were dark, except beneath her wings. When she moved, the feathers sparkled like starlight. Compared to normal birds, she looked like a fancy bird queen.

"Novi, as in . . . the legendary beast known only in myths and legends?" Setia asked.

Argo just smiled.

"She's pretty. Is she special?" Varric asked. Novi turned her hawk-like glare on him. He decided not to get too close.

"Not just special, but one of a kind." Setia pressed the heel of her palm to her forehead. "It's supposedly impossible for humans to approach her. Argo, how did you . . . Who are you?"

"Hear how special you are, girl?" Argo nuzzled Novi's head against his own. She hummed in pleasure and returned the gesture. He said, "Thanks for the help, as always. Away you go."

Novi imploded in a flash of light and disappeared from the realm.

"Why not keep her out? We could fly and look around," Varric said, a little disappointed. Even if she wanted to peck out his eyes, she was cool. And flying was great—much better than plummeting to his death.

"She's powerful, so it takes a lot of energy to keep her here." Argo ran a hand through his hair, which had gotten pretty disheveled during their flight. "I can keep her around for a while, but I'd rather save my strength in case we find trouble."

"That's fair. It's the same for my wings," Setia said. "No point in wasting energy if we're staying on the ground." She shrugged her shoulders, and her wings disappeared in a flash. She turned a stern look on Varric, but he saw a hint of concern behind it. "I know you couldn't reveal to them that you're an Interloper, but why didn't you teleport away and save yourself?"

"I was falling. If I teleported, I'd still be falling. I'd splat on the ground wherever I went," Varric explained. "I was trying to think of deep water, but I couldn't concentrate while that thing kept attacking me."

"It didn't hurt you?" Argo asked. He looked Varric over to check for himself.

"No. It seemed like it was trying to catch me. I don't think it meant for me to fall."

Argo and Setia exchanged looks. Only then did Varric recognize the oddity of his statement. What would a Wasteling want with him?

"Now that we're here, we should look around," Setia said. "Let's figure out why the people of Clobalt pretend this place doesn't exist. I bet our Wasteling thief is around here."

"And hopefully the relic, too." Varric wagged his explosive-bound wrist in the air. "I'm ready to get rid of this thing."

"Let's have a look around then, shall we?" Argo nodded at them and led the way through the wastes.

Chapter 8
Knoll of the Wastes

"Argh. This place is huge. We'll never find anything." Varric kicked a clump of dark soil into the sludge. The dirt made a few bubbles before sinking.

They'd walked for what felt like hours on pathways of dirt surrounded by bubbling black goo. The scenery never changed. Varric ate his leftover meat and vegetable skewer. When he finished, he tossed the stick and wrapper into the sludge. They sizzled and melted instantly. A few angry bubbles burped to the surface along with a puff of smoke. Varric stopped and stared. Setia and Argo did, too.

"Don't fall in," Argo suggested.

"What if the Wastelings are in the sludge?" Varric asked as they resumed walking. "What if they're here, but we can't see them? There's too much ground to cover to just wander around aimlessly."

"For once, I agree with you," Setia said. Light flashed at her back, and her white wings unfurled. A few feathers fluttered into the sludge and burned up. "I'm going to look around."

"Be careful up there. If you see anything suspicious, get back here," Argo said, crossing his arms. Setia raised an eyebrow at him, causing him to shrug. "What? Your dad would have my head if I brought you back in pieces."

"I'll be fine." Setia squinted at him like she wasn't sure what to make of his concern. Then she took to the air, wings fluttering. "Be back soon." With that, she soared away.

Varric watched her until she faded into the hazy smoke. Sighing, he wandered the area where he and Argo waited. He checked his pouch to see if he had anything else to throw in the sludge, but he only had the ring from Clobalt. He thought about throwing that in, but he should probably return it.

It didn't take long for Setia to return, zipping in their direction with her wings beating furiously. She swooped down and landed hard, sliding through the dirt.

"I found them," she said, pointing in the direction she'd come from. "A lot of Wastelings. They saw me but didn't follow."

"The relic must be here!" Varric bounced on the tips of his boots. "I'll teleport us as far as I can see. Let's go!"

Setia flew and pointed out patches of ground within Varric's eyesight. He teleported himself and Argo to wherever she pointed, traveling a large distance in minimal time. They did that for a while, though, and Varric got dizzy and hungry from teleporting so much. It was more difficult when bringing someone with him, but he wanted to hurry and find the relic so they could get out of there. Maybe someone would buy him more food once they found the relic.

After teleporting to the next patch of ground, Argo grabbed Varric's arm to stop him. Setia landed nearby, pointing down a path to a swarm of giant bugs. The beasts fluttered around, the beats of their wings droning in the air. Setia summoned her spear as they jogged down the path toward the beasts.

"Is that a person with them?" Varric asked.

He thought he saw a human shape among them when the Wastelings swarmed in certain directions. The human shape became clearer the closer they got, and they slowed their jog to a rapid walk.

"I didn't notice before," Setia admitted.

Argo led the way to a wide plot of land where the Wastelings gathered. There had to be at least fifty of the creatures. The Wastelings fluttered aside and revealed a man dressed in sleek dark clothes with a cloak and hood. The dark clothes contrasted his light skin, pale eyes, and white hair, which hung over his shoulder in a twisty bundle. Aside from the less-crazy hairstyle and dark clothes, he looked similar to the rest of the people of Clobalt. He sat on a big, bumpy chair that looked like a throne, and the chair appeared to be moving. No, it was moving! Wastelings had linked their bodies together to form the chair, and sometimes a wing, leg, or hooked tail popped out!

"Welcome to my domain," the man exclaimed in a cheerful voice, extending his arms wide in greeting.

"You live here?" Varric asked, grimacing at the creepiness of the living chair. He wondered if the guy was getting poked by bug legs.

"Of course. It's such a lovely place," the man said.

"Who are you?" Setia gripped her spear in both hands and slipped one foot forward.

"You come to my abode and demand my name? Undeniably rude and unbecoming."

"You're weird," Varric said.

"Bonus points for honesty." The man shook a finger at Varric. "My name is Knoll, former citizen of Clobalt, present citizen of the wastes. Who are you?" After Setia gave him their first names, he continued, "And what brings you to my homeland? Few make it here alive, you know."

"We're looking for a Wasteling that stole a relic from Iloria," Varric said, figuring there was no point avoiding the truth. Either the guy could help them or he couldn't. "Have you seen anything like that?"

The Wastelings, even those that made up the chair, started hissing. Their bulging eyes locked on Varric. They clicked their mandibles at him, and some jerked their tails forward like they intended to stab him. Argo positioned himself ahead of Varric, shielding him with his body. Setia's eyes narrowed as they scanned the swarm of Wastelings.

"They don't seem to like you much." Knoll chuckled at Varric.

"I get that a lot."

"Might be the smell . . ." Knoll tapped his nose, his grin showing straight, white teeth.

"I don't smell as bad as this place," Varric muttered, tired of people grumbling about his hygiene.

"Depends on who you ask." Knoll slid out of his weird, living chair and stood tall, stretching his long arms above his head. "As for your question, yes, I know the Ethari you seek."

"Ethari?" Setia echoed, and she exchanged puzzled glances with Varric and Argo.

Knoll stared at them like they were idiots and then muttered under his breath to the Wastelings. The beasts clicked their mandibles in reply, and Knoll nodded like he understood what they were saying.

"Humans are so uncivilized," Knoll said, extending his arms to present the Wastelings behind him. "These collective creatures you ignorantly call 'beasts' are known as Ethari. Just as humans come in a variety of shapes, sizes, and colors, so the Ethari come in various forms."

"I've never heard the word 'Ethari' before," Setia said.

"And surely that means it can't be true?" Knoll glared at Setia, who shifted under his intense focus. "Ethari were once proud beings full of ancient magic. Humans grew envious of their magic and banished them from the realms until only a few remained. Then they relegated the Ethari to the status of mindless beasts to cover their own heinous acts."

"History disagrees. The beasts attacked us," Setia said. "We banished them to the realm of Radomere to keep them from destroying us. They were the aggressors, not humans."

"Whatever you tell yourself to sleep at night, little girl," Knoll said in a sing-song voice.

Setia opened her mouth like she was about to argue, but Argo set a hand on her upper arm.

"About the Wasteling with the relic?" Argo asked.

"I saw the relic," Knoll said. "The Ethari you seek already left this realm for another, and he took the relic with him."

"Where did he go?" Varric stepped out from behind Argo, ignoring the hostility the Wastelings showed him.

"I know, of course. But I won't tell you." Knoll giggled behind his hand and then flopped down into his chair made of Wastelings, sitting sideways with his legs folded over one of the arms.

"Please!" Varric took a step forward. The Wastelings hissed, but he didn't care. "We need the relic. It's very important."

"What do you suppose an Ethari would want with the relic?" Knoll flapped a hand over his mouth as he yawned.

"To see whatever it desires?" Varric grumbled.

"Is that all you humans think the relic is capable of? Finding an item you fancy? Truly?" Knoll scoffed. "The relic is a key, you barbarians. It's made of ancient magic capable of opening an ancient magical door." He crossed one leg over the other and waited for a reaction. When they gave none, he sighed and threw his hands into the air. "It opens a door to a being more powerful than you could imagine: the Sage of Wind."

"I've never heard of this," Setia muttered. Her eyebrow twitched like she was mentally arguing with herself whether to believe him or not.

"Of course not," Knoll said. "The humans who hid the Wind Sage never meant for her to be retrieved. They hid the key relic within the realms, and its original purpose was intentionally concealed and eventually forgotten. No one wanted the Sage to be found."

"What does the Wind Sage do?" Varric asked. Excitement stirred in his belly. Maybe that was why Jonavad wanted the relic. Maybe the Wind Sage had the power to save his mom.

Knoll grinned. "The Sage of Wind is capable of changing the foundations of our realms in disastrous ways. Ways that could undo the realms themselves." He patted another nearby Wasteling. "Now what would an Ethari do with such magic against the human realms that have tormented the Ethari for centuries? Curious, yes?"

"Such a thing can't exist," Setia said. She shook her head, but her voice wavered. "My family would know the purpose of our relic."

"Yes, because you certainly know everything, don't you?" Knoll propped his head in his hand. "You don't have to believe me. Go ahead and let the Wasteling release the Sage. It's no skin off my back. Power to him. I hope he puts you humans in your place."

"You realize you're human too, right?" Varric asked.

"Am I?" Knoll snorted. "My fellow Clobaltians didn't think so when they threw me over the edge of their floating city and let me plummet to my death."

"What?" Varric exclaimed, and Setia covered her mouth with her hand.

"Oh, they didn't tell you?" Knoll feigned a shocked expression before rolling his eyes. "What a surprise. Get on their wrong side and they'll throw you to your death."

"What did you do?" Varric asked, which drew a fit of laughter from Knoll.

"Oh, they had their reasons. One being that I questioned the treatment of Brightlings enslaved throughout the city. That's what pushed them to take action against me. They plotted to take my ring so the realm would destroy me. I knew they would, so I stole another and wore it on my necklace." Knoll pulled a leather necklace out from under his shirt, revealing a ring similar to the ones they'd been provided. "Sure enough, they took me captive, confiscated the ring off my finger, and threw me over the edge."

Grabbing a Wasteling, he snuggled it like a kitten. Considering it was a giant bug, Varric's nose crinkled.

Knoll continued, "The Ethari took pity on me and rescued me as I fell. Few others have been quite so lucky. Let me guess. The Clobaltians told you nothing existed below the clouds." When they nodded, Knoll said, "They're lying. They know what's down here. They built their city here, after all, many, many moons ago. Do you know why they lifted their city into the sky?"

"No, but I bet you'll tell us," Varric said, because the guy loved talking.

Knoll grinned, big and wide. "They were fleeing."

Massive eruptions of sludge punctuated his statement. Over thirty creatures as big as houses surged out of the swamps.

They looked like crabs, with jointed legs, pincers for arms, and shells covered in jagged spikes. The worst part about them was their eyes—they didn't have any. Instead, they only had empty black holes in their heads.

The crab creatures scuttled out of the sludge and surrounded Varric and his allies.

Chapter 9

Who is this Man?

C rab creatures surrounded them. Most stayed at a slight
distance, but there was no way around them, not
without flying or teleporting, at least. Setia pranced on her
toes, squeezing her spear in both hands. Argo held a protective
arm in front of Varric, not that there was much he could do
against all those huge creatures.

Knoll laughed. "The Ethari reclaimed the realm and sent the
humans cowering into the sky. Isn't that amusing?"

"Not right now, it isn't," Varric murmured.

He scooted closer to Argo and desperately wished he had his
dagger. If he had Valkaris, he could send the beasts away with
a tiny poke. He could teleport them, but it would take a lot of
energy, and he was already tired and hungry. And where would
he send them? He couldn't send them to Radomere without
Valkaris, and he didn't want to send them somewhere with
people.

"Tell you what. I do like to give everyone a fair chance."
Knoll twirled his hair on his finger. "Defeat twenty of my

companions here, and I'll tell you where to find your little lost relic."

"That's fair?" Setia snapped. "These things are massive."

"Fair-ish." Knoll shrugged. "Go get 'em!"

The crab beasts—Varric decided to call them Crablings—scuttled toward them, their jointed legs splashing through the sludge.

"Can't you send them away like you did in Iloria?" Setia asked Varric.

"Not without my dagger," Varric said. "And I definitely can't get rid of this many. Even I have my limits."

Argo grabbed the back of Varric's cloak and shuffled him toward Setia. He said, "Setia, protect him. Varric, be prepared to get us out of here if things get bad. You can handle teleporting the three of us, yeah?" When Varric nodded, Argo continued, "That's the plan."

"What plan?" Setia asked breathlessly.

"Come forth, Cerbrus and Novi," Argo summoned.

Lights flashed on either side of him, forcing Varric and Setia to move aside. Two creatures burst into existence. One was the starlight bird called Novi, who perched on Argo's back like before so he could use her wings. The other creature was a giant dog with skin like clusters of dark stone and ice with veins of blue light shining through the cracks. Its eyes blazed blue, its ears stood straight up and alert, its fierce claws hooked into the dirt, and its curled lips revealed rows of pearly white fangs. It had a nubbin for a tail.

"That's another legendary beast! Cerbrus, the king of the iciest, deadliest mountains in Yerevir," Setia exclaimed. "Who is this man?"

A flash of light ignited from Argo's leather bracer, and a battle ax formed in his outstretched hand. It was mostly silver but had a rainbow gleam on the sharp edges of its blades. Like Varric's dagger, the grip was elaborate black and silver. Argo swung the weapon downward, creating a shockwave that stirred the dirt.

"Time to play, my friends," Argo called to his two beast companions.

Novi unleashed a warbling cry and Cerbrus howled. Cerbrus tackled the nearest Crabling and rolled on the ground with it. He bit the Crabling's pincer arm and shook the beast like a ragdoll before hurling it into the distance. The dog beast jumped on the swamp, and the black sludge solidified into ice around his paws.

Meanwhile, Argo took to the air with Novi, plummeting on top of the nearest Crabling. He swung down his ax on the beast's black shell. As soon as the rainbow edge of his ax made contact, the Crabling imploded into a portal and disappeared.

"It's the same as my dagger," Varric exclaimed. He'd always thought his weapon was one of a kind. "He's sending them to Radomere."

"I knew this was going to be exciting." Knoll clapped his hands and then chewed on his nails. "Oh dear. Whatever will happen?"

Most of the Crablings focused on attacking Argo, Novi, and Cerbrus, but several scuttled past them, approaching Varric and Setia. Setia leaped into the air and thrust her spear at one of the Crablings. No matter how many times she got close, it swiped its pincers and forced her into evasive maneuvers. Her wings seemed to move intuitively, because she weaved and dodged in ways that didn't match her stabbing moves.

Varric scooted backward and wished he had a weapon. Anything would have been useful at that point. He hated feeling useless.

A Crabling lunged out of the swamp at Setia. Varric teleported the jumping Crabling to the other side of the wastes, because he didn't know where else to put it. Exhaustion pummeled him from the effort. His body got heavy, his mind got foggy, and his stomach rumbled. The bigger the object, the harder it was for him to move. Meanwhile, several more Crablings scurried out of the wastes and forced Setia back. She landed beside Varric. Her wings dissolved and sweat soaked her face. She'd been using her magic for a long time, so her strength must have run out. Still, she held her spear forward as several more Crablings swarmed them.

Cerbrus howled and pounced on the sludge, sending out a pulse of frigid wind and snowflakes. Ice spread over the land and froze the Crablings that were half-submerged. Right afterward, Cerbrus disappeared. Varric assumed that meant Argo ran out of the strength to keep him in the realm. Argo darted over as many frozen Crablings as he could, hitting them with his ax. Then Novi vanished from his back. He rolled on the ground and popped to one knee, his ax held ready. Sweat drenched his hair and clothes.

"All right. That's enough." Knoll clapped his hands.

The Crablings crawled back into the deep swamp and ducked out of sight, leaving bubbles and plumes of smoke behind.

"That was way more than twenty," Argo muttered, glaring at Knoll. He dropped his ax, and it disappeared before it hit the dirt.

"Bonus points. I'll give you an extra tip for your effort. Thanks for the entertainment."

"You don't seem to care much about these so-called Ethari if you're willing to kill them for entertainment." Setia swiped her hand across her sweaty forehead. Her spear disappeared.

"Kill them? They didn't die, did they?" Knoll entwined his fingers, stretched his arms ahead of him, and cracked all his fingers at once. "The man sent them to another realm with his ax. The boy sent them to the other side of this realm. Neither harmed them."

"Cerbrus and I hurt them." Setia glared at him.

"Their legs grow back." Knoll shrugged. "And you poked them. I would have stopped you if you'd killed them." Leaning forward on his seat, he set an elbow on his knee and propped his head in his hand. "What an interesting bunch, though. A Bonder with two legendary Ethari. A Shifter who can fight. And a little baby Interloper. How unlikely."

"I'm not little," Varric grumbled. The heat rushing to his cheeks only made him dizzier.

Knoll's eyes twinkled. He sat back in his Wasteling seat and let out a belly laugh.

"We played your game." Argo stood and seemed to have caught his breath. He was still a mess, though. Some areas of his clothes had been torn or burned, like the Crablings had snipped him with their pincers or he'd been splashed with swamp acid. "What do you know about the location of Iloria's relic?"

"The Sage's gate that the relic opens is located in a realm called Khalkar."

"Never heard of it," Setia muttered.

"Few have," Knoll said. "There's no known portal that will lead humans there."

"So the beast can't get there, either?" Varric asked.

"Ethari. Not beast." Knoll grinned, totally smug. "And I assume he'll find a way. There are ways between the realms if you're clever enough to find them."

"Do you want the Wasteling to release the Sage?" Argo asked.

Knoll shrugged. "I just love a good game. To the victor go the spoils and all that." His eyes flashed, and his lips curled into a feral smile. "Although I would love to see you humans get what's coming to you."

"And what's coming to us?" Setia asked.

"Revenge," Knoll said with a light laugh. "Find Khalkar, and you'll find the relic. If the Wasteling hasn't already released the Sage, that is. Once the Sage is free, you humans are in trouble."

"You're a human," Varric reminded him.

"Am I?" Knoll checked his fingernails, his eyebrows arching under his tousled hair.

"This guy is crazy." Varric rubbed his aching head.

"Let's head back to Iloria and ask Bernadea if she knows anything about Khalkar and this Sage," Setia whispered.

"Agreed," Argo said. "Varric, can you take us there?"

"Yeah, easy." Varric returned his attention to Knoll. "Thanks for the unpleasant experience. And the info, I guess."

"No problem, little boy Interloper." Knoll's gaze lingered on Varric with an uncomfortable intensity—so intense that Argo stepped forward like he expected Knoll to attack. Knoll glanced at Argo before shifting his eyes back to Varric. "I would be sorely disappointed if this was our last meeting. Do be safe out there in the many realms, please."

Varric shuffled uncomfortably, making Knoll grin.

"Oh, and I promised a bonus tip!" Knoll winked. "You'll want to consider the Blushing Pond."

"Which is?" Argo asked.

"I didn't say I'd explain the tip. Just that I'd give it." Knoll stuck out his tongue and pulled down the bottom lid of one eye. "Off you go. The little boy Interloper smells foul, and my companions don't like it."

The Wastelings broke into a fit of raspy, creepy laughter, their wings fluttering and mandibles clicking.

"You smell foul—" Varric started, but Argo grabbed him with an arm around his shoulders.

"Let's get out of here," Argo said.

Varric teleported away with Argo and Setia. Knoll's laughter echoed after them.

Chapter 10

Digging for Secrets

Varric teleported them a short distance from Bernadea's gate. He didn't want to teleport too close in case her gate panel was watching. The sun was well past midday, warm and turning a little orange as it lowered toward the horizon. A breeze rustled the grass and leaves of the nearby trees. He strolled over to the gate, excited to push the button.

"I'll admit your powers do come in handy," Setia said, walking alongside him. When he reached for the button, she grabbed his arm. "Wait! What are we going to tell her?"

"The truth?" Varric raised an eyebrow.

"Do we even know the truth? Knoll didn't seem that trustworthy," Setia said.

"But it's the only information we have right now," Argo said. "We need to share what we know so Bernadea can look into it. The more information, the better."

"Fine." Setia released Varric and rubbed her forehead. "I just hope I don't make my family look crazy."

"Don't worry." Varric wagged his explosive bracelet. "Your family already looks crazy."

Setia glared at him and stabbed the button with her finger before Varric could.

"Hey!" he whined. "It was my turn."

"Child," Setia muttered under her breath, but she bit back a smirk at the same time. It twinkled in her eyes.

Crashes erupted from the gate panel, followed by some screeching sounds like metal on metal.

"Who bothers me?" Bernadea shouted from the panel. "What do you want?"

An image displayed on the panel of Bernadea soaked in sweat, her hair buns all disheveled. She crouched in front of a bar with metal slabs on either side, lifted it off the ground, and hoisted it over her head. Then she returned it to the ground and did it again, gasping for air between lifts.

"You can't look much crazier than her, anyway," Varric muttered out of the corner of his mouth. Setia ignored him, but Argo grinned.

"It's Princess Setia," Setia said.

"Again?" Bernadea lifted the bar with an agonizing groan. She sounded like she was dying. "I just helped you. You didn't need to return to thank me. Truly. Go away."

"We have more questions," Setia said.

"Important questions," Varric added. "Like, realm-ending important."

"That's what they always say." Bernadea set down the bar and gasped for air.

"It's true, Bernadea. It's incredibly important." Setia leaned closer to the panel. "Please do this as a favor to me."

"Fine, come in. Hurry it up." Bernadea's picture vanished from the panel.

The gate creaked open, and Varric and the others entered. The little garden rodents trundled through the grass, making things fancy and pristine along the way. Varric wondered what would happen if he sat in front of one. Would it try to pick him up or chop him up like twigs that fell in the yard? They entered through the sliding doors and found Bernadea still hard at work lifting her weights. As they passed the crystal with the captive Waveling, the beast locked its eyes on Varric, bared its fangs, and violently thrashed against the crystal walls. Varric moved so that Argo was between him and the crystal.

"Beasts don't like you, do they?" Setia asked.

"I don't know why." Varric scowled and sniffed his cloak on his shoulder. It wasn't like the beast in the crystal could smell him. Shaking off the frustration of constantly being hated by everyone, he distracted himself with Bernadea's bizarre antics. "What are you doing?"

"Building muscle mass." She squatted and hoisted up the bar with a scream like she was being murdered. "Keeps the burn going longer!"

"Your form is off," Argo said, rubbing his facial scruff. "That's bad for your back."

Bernadea dropped the bar on the floor with a loud clang. Considering how heavy it sounded, Varric was surprised it didn't dent the tile. The old lady glared at Argo, who offered his usual charming smile.

"Don't smile at me, you oversized piece of meat." Bernadea waved him away, growling. "Men have it so easy. All height and muscle. You probably burn more energy sleeping for one night than I do exercising all week." Grabbing two miniature exercise bars similar to the big one she'd dropped, she curled them to her shoulders, one in each hand. "Not fair, you know. Sometimes I'd like to eat cake."

"Bernadea, what do you know about the realm of Khalkar?" Setia asked, all business.

"Never heard of it."

"The Sage of Wind?" Argo tried.

"Are you making things up?" She threw in some leg squats with her arm curls. "Never heard of that, either."

"Ethari?" Varric asked.

"Are you playing with me? What's this all about?" Bernadea dropped her exercise bars on the floor and stood with her hands on her hips.

"We're being honest. Can you look these things up for us? Please?" Setia gestured toward the tech device and tray of buttons Bernadea had used during their last visit.

"Khalkar, you said?" Bernadea sighed and trudged over to the device, pulling up a chair she only partly sat on. She poked a few buttons, and the panel flashed with a variety of letters Varric didn't understand. "Nothing."

"What about Ethari or the Sage of Wind?" Varric grabbed the short exercise bars and curled them the way she had.

"Get your grubby little fingers off my dumbbells," Bernadea muttered without even looking, and he scurried to return them to their original place. "And no. I see nothing about any of those things in the common info-bases."

"Maybe he really was lying." Setia rubbed her forehead.

"He, who?" Bernadea swiveled the top of her chair to face Setia.

"Knoll," Varric said. "Some guy the Clobaltians threw off their city. He lives in the wastes."

Bernadea swiveled around in his direction, her eyes bulging out of her head, looking extra big and bug-eyed through her glasses. "Did you say the wastes?"

"Y-yes?"

"You met a man from there?"

"Yeah," Varric said, glancing at his comrades to make sure it was okay to talk about it. Neither made any indication he should stop. "We fell off the floating city and found him living below."

"You've been to the wastes?" Bernadea leaped from her chair and grabbed Varric's shoulders. "You've seen them with your own eyes?"

"If you smell us, you can probably still smell the wastes on us," Argo said. His eyebrows shot up when she grabbed the edge of Varric's cloak, took a deep sniff, and started coughing. Varric's cheeks burned.

"We spoke with Knoll in the wastes. Is this important?" Setia asked.

"Beyond important!" Bernadea's cough turned into a cackle. "Don't you understand? The wastes have been a thing of legend for centuries. I had to dig through ancient information to even learn it existed. Clobalt tried so hard to hide it. How nice to have my searches confirmed. You must tell me about it. Tell me everything." Bernadea plopped into her swivel chair, kicking her feet like a little kid ready for story time. "Do you have detailed maps? Did you bring anything back?"

"Nothing besides the smell," Argo commented, shrugging.

Bernadea sank and blew out a breath through mostly closed lips. She looked like she'd give anything for details on the wasteland, which to Varric hadn't been exciting at all. But if it was a mysterious place she could only study through uncommon information, he understood. Then an idea hit him.

"You said you looked through common info for Khalkar and the other things we mentioned, right?" he asked. "I'm guessing you didn't find out about Clobalt's wastes through common info, did you? You had to dig deeper to find it . . ."

"Maybe I did." Bernadea squinted at him. Her eyes shot to Setia, and Varric realized why Bernadea didn't look in those uncommon places for them.

Setia realized it, too. She crossed her arms and looked aside. "You found out about Clobalt's wastes through less-than-legal methods, didn't you? If you use those methods to help us, I won't hold anything against you."

"I don't know what methods you're talking about." Bernadea grabbed the edge of her table and swiveled her chair around in circles.

"If you look a little deeper for information about Khalkar, Ethari, and the Wind Sage, we'll tell you everything we know about the wastes of Clobalt," Varric said. "Including everything we learned from Knoll and about the beasts we saw there—"

"You saw beasts?" Bernadea halted her swiveling, and her eyes lit up.

"Wastelings and Crablings."

"Crablings?" Argo raised an eyebrow, but Varric waved at him to be quiet.

"Never heard of them." Bernadea rubbed her chin, eyeballing each of them in turn—especially Setia, since she had the power to get Bernadea in trouble.

"I promise I won't say anything," Setia said. "Please help us. A lot more might be at stake than just my family's relic."

"Fine. I'll do it." Bernadea turned back to her tech device. "It'll take a while. Come back tomorrow afternoon. Shoo." She set to work poking away at her buttons.

Varric and the others shuffled toward the door. The Waveling in the crystal jumped at him again, making him scamper behind Argo. The beast thrashed and clawed the crystal walls.

"Pipe down over there," Bernadea scolded. "Why do you keep riling up the Waveling?"

"All I'm doing is existing and it's getting riled up," Varric muttered.

"Let's head back to Iloria City and stay the night," Setia said as they stepped out the automatic doors. "I could use a hot bath and a warm meal. We can stay at the castle."

"No, thanks," Varric said.

"Why not?"

"I don't really want to hang out in a place where they thought it was fun to put an explosive on me. Nothing better than roaming around a castle where everyone knows you're a criminal, hates you, and wants you executed."

"No one would hurt you," Setia assured him, her face twisting in sorrow. She looked genuinely hurt that he felt that way about her home and family, but he couldn't help it.

Varric softened his voice. "Still, no thanks." He did appreciate her offer, at least. They stepped beyond Bernadea's front gate, and he led them to the shaded area near the trees where he felt safe using his powers.

"Varric and I can stay at the inn. They have baths, and we can grab food from the tavern," Argo said.

"Are you sure?" Setia stopped under the trees, frowning, clearly bothered by the whole situation. When Argo and Varric nodded, she pulled a jingling satchel out of her belt pouch. "Then use this."

"I have my own gold," Argo said, though he took it. Varric eyed the satchel, which sounded pretty full of jinglies.

"I'll take it if you don't want it," Varric said, only slightly teasing.

"You're both doing Iloria a service by helping find the relic. Even you, Varric, despite your circumstances. I appreciate it." Setia squared her shoulders. "If Knoll is telling the truth, there's a lot more going on than we realize. This might be about more than Iloria. We need to find out what's going on. Until then, I appreciate your continued support."

"I'm not going anywhere," Argo said, nodding.

"I don't have a choice either way." Varric waved his bracelet. When Setia's face crumpled, guilt blossomed in his chest. He offered an apologetic smile. "I guess I'd probably keep helping even without the bracelet, though."

Actually, he was sure he would. Not only did he need to save his mom, but if the Wind Sage could destroy realms, he couldn't let that happen. He'd already watched his own realm get destroyed, and he wouldn't go through that again.

"Thank you." Setia set her hand on Varric's shoulder, squeezing. "I'll speak to my father about the explosive device and see if he'll remove it."

"Could you also ask him for my dagger?" Varric asked, feeling a surge of excitement. "It would let me be more helpful."

"I'll try. I'll also ask him if he knows anything about what Knoll mentioned. Perhaps he can provide additional guidance in case Bernadea doesn't learn anything."

"If Bernadea doesn't figure it out, I doubt anyone will," Argo said. He patted Varric and Setia on the back. "Let's go, shall we? I'm getting hungry after all that playing we did in the wastes . . . with the *Crablings*."

"Crablings." Setia let out a puff of air and rolled her eyes.

"It's not any worse than Wastelings," Varric said, grinning. "I thought it was pretty clever."

Setia shook her head. "Just take us to Iloria City, would you?"

Chapter 11

I'm not a Thief!

Varric sat in the corner on the floor and ate a meat bun Argo had purchased for him. He watched as Argo cleaned the blades of his big battle ax. They'd spent the morning hours roaming Iloria City and had returned to the inn to wait for Setia. Like all the other places in the city, the inn was made of wood and stone and had lots of trees and plants growing in, around, and through it. Varric finished his meat bun and contemplated eating something else, but he decided to save his leftovers. Argo had bought him quite a few packable breads, jerky, and dried fruits. Varric felt bad taking so much stuff for himself, but it was hard to pass up good food.

"Do you have an Orbeel that holds your ax like Setia's?" Varric slid up the wall so he could get a better look at Argo's fancy weapon.

"Yes." Argo raised his arm to show a green Orbeel set in his leather bracer. "Works the same way."

"If something happened to you, would anyone get the ax back?" Varric reworded the question he'd unsuccessfully asked Setia.

"If the user dies, the Orbeel expels the weapon and disconnects from it," Argo said. "Someone else can then claim the weapon and Orbeel, using them as their own."

"Cool. I want one."

Varric shuffled a little closer to where Argo sat on the bed with one foot braced against a stool, his ax propped on his bent leg. The ax looked like something that belonged in a castle—maybe even with the best knight in the realm. No, with a member of the royal family, or as a decoration on the wall behind their throne.

"It's a really nice ax. What's it called?"

"Randagar."

"You named it!" Varric plopped down on the bed beside Argo. His dagger had a name, but he didn't know many other weapons that did.

"It had a name before I received it." Argo grinned. "It was named after the person who originally wielded it."

"Where'd you get it from?"

"A good friend gave it to me."

"A birthday present?"

"More like an unexpected farewell present." Argo ran his hand along the edge of one blade, leaned forward to inspect it, and then set his cleaning fabric aside.

"Did your friend die?" Varric asked, not realizing how rude it sounded until Argo stopped and stared at him.

Rather than becoming upset, Argo smiled, his face and eyes full of warmth. Varric squirmed under the attention. Argo shook off his stare and inhaled deeply. He returned his attention to his ax, the warmth melting away, replaced by grief and sorrow.

"Yeah, he did," Argo said.

"Sorry."

Varric kicked his feet over the side of the bed and dropped his gaze to the floor. It was a dumb question, and he shouldn't have asked. Before he could stress over it, Argo smiled and ruffled his hair, so it was probably okay.

A knock on the door saved Varric from accidentally asking any more dumb questions.

"Argo? Varric?" Setia's voice passed through the wood.

"We're in here." Argo made his ax disappear.

"We should get moving. I'll be waiting outside," Setia said. Her footsteps thudded against the wooden boards and went down the hallway.

Varric and Argo gathered their things and headed down the hall to the main entrance of the inn. They pushed past a few guests clustered near the counter and exited to the shadowy main street of Iloria City. Setia waited under the light of one of the crystal streetlamps. She opened her mouth like she intended to greet them, but her eyes narrowed on Varric.

"You didn't take a bath?" Her glare shifted to Argo. "Why didn't he take a bath?"

Argo shrugged. "He didn't want to."

"I washed up my own way," Varric snapped at Setia, irritated that the first thing she said was about how he looked. He could have used the baths at the inn like Argo, but he didn't like taking off his things. Unattached things could be stolen.

"Did you use soap?" Setia leaned closer and sniffed him. Her nose crinkled.

"A little. Maybe." Varric huffed. He'd gone to his usual spot for bathing, a river in another realm. He'd stored some supplies near the river since no one knew about the place, but his soap had gotten a little dry and crusty.

"And you didn't change your clothes," she said, her frown deepening. Only then did he notice that she'd changed into an even fancier tunic and leather gear.

"What does it matter to you?" he grumbled, more and more irritated. She seemed to care more about how he looked and smelled than the fact that he'd tried to steal Iloria's relic.

"It matters because you'll draw unwanted attention to yourself—"

"To you, you mean," Varric snapped, his hands clenched into fists at his sides. "You're worried about you. Not me."

"I am worried about you." Setia crossed her arms. "You'll better convince my father and others that you aren't a thief if you don't look and play the role of thief so perfectly. I gave Argo plenty of gold. You could have at least bought new clothes."

"I don't want new clothes."

"You're impossible." Setia threw up her hands and turned to Argo, looking him over. "I see you changed clothes."

"My old ones are being repaired. I'll grab them next time we're in town." Argo adjusted the rolled-up sleeves of his new shirt.

His new shirt and pants were black like the last ones. Varric couldn't help but think he was dressing shady for a reason.

Setia led the way down the street toward the city gates, to places where Varric could safely use his powers. Most of the tourists from the Tournament had left Iloria, so it was a lot quieter. Some of the market vendors were still up and running, selling food and clothing, but other stalls had packed up and departed. Lots of people stared at them as they passed. No, they stared at Varric. He made sure his explosive bracelet was covered by his cloak. They kept staring. Feeling self-conscious, he scooted between Argo and Setia, hoping to cover some of his feral features. He tried to organize his hair, but it was a tangled mess and a lost cause. Instead, he pulled up his hood. Maybe he did need a bath so he wouldn't stand out so much.

They passed through the city gates. Varric led them into a cluster of trees where he could teleport without being seen by the city guards at the gate.

"Hold up." Setia pulled the Clobaltian ring off her finger and offered it to Varric. "Can you return these to Clobalt?"

"Right now? Why?" he asked.

"Because they don't belong to us and we should have returned them right away."

"The people of Clobalt probably think we're dead." Varric took the ring anyway and pulled his own from his belt pouch. Argo gave Varric his ring.

"It doesn't matter. It's the right thing to do," Setia said. "Do you still have the glider?"

"It ripped and fell off when I was falling," Varric admitted.

"We left ours on the platform when we flew down to rescue you," Argo explained.

"So you don't have to worry about returning those." Setia set her hands on her hips and waited.

Varric sighed at the demands. For someone who hated his magic and how illegal it was, she sure liked to put him to use.

"You don't have to personally return them," she said. "Just leave them somewhere where they'll be found."

"You're demanding. Definitely a princess," Varric grumbled.

He teleported into the room with the portal station in Clobalt. Since Clobalt rarely had guests, he assumed people wouldn't be in the room. He was right. The room was dark besides a few stray lights falling in through the high windows. He set the rings on top of the panel that controlled the inactive portal station. Then he teleported back to his allies.

"Did you return them? Where did you leave them?" Setia asked, her eyes narrowing. "That didn't take long."

"Yeah, I brought them back," Varric snapped. "I put them on the panel by the portal station." When she continued glaring at him, anger curled in his belly. "I'm telling the truth. I didn't steal them."

"If it makes you feel better," Argo said, nudging Setia with his elbow, "I left the bag of gold in our room when I went to the baths. Kid didn't take a single coin."

"You were testing me?" Varric stepped back, feeling betrayed by both of them. He hadn't tried to steal anything from either of them in the time they'd been together.

"No," Argo said, "but I realized after the fact and checked the gold to satisfy my curiosity."

"I'm not a thief!" Varric's fists trembled at his sides. The frustration in his chest grew and hot tears prickled his eyes. What he said wasn't entirely honest. He'd tried to steal the relic. But he really did do his best not to steal much. Taking from others hurt them, and he didn't want to hurt people. "I mean, sometimes I have to steal to eat, but only little stuff. I wasn't there to steal the relic so I could sell it for gold. I tried to steal it because—" Varric slapped his hands over his mouth, realizing he'd said too much.

Argo and Setia's eyes were wide open.

"Why did you try to steal the relic?" Argo asked softly.

"What do you need it for?" Setia sounded as curious as Argo, but a little less gentle about it. Still, there wasn't much judgment in her voice anymore.

"Look, never mind. Just stop calling me a thief." Varric rubbed the explosive bracelet and then held it toward Setia. "Did you even ask your dad to remove this?"

Setia hesitated. "He declined."

"And my dagger?"

"I'm sorry, Varric." Setia set her hand on his outstretched arm, but he withdrew it and tucked it under his cloak. "He said he needs the relic first."

"Of course he did."

"I also mentioned what Knoll said. My father said none of it mattered besides the relic. I don't think he believed me."

"Let's hope Bernadea comes up with something that will lead us to the relic." Argo squeezed Varric's shoulder. "We still have some leads to follow. We'll find the relic and get that bracelet off you."

Varric nodded, but he wasn't too optimistic. They were already on day five. Almost half of his two-week time limit had passed. Were they crazy for chasing a beast around the realms? Was there any chance they'd find it? It could hide in places like the wastes of Clobalt that people didn't even realize existed. But he couldn't give up. If the bracelet exploded, who would save his mom? Who would give a better life to his baby sisters? He caused all their problems in the first place, and he owed it to his family to fix them.

Varric teleported them straight into Bernadea's front yard, past the gate and guest-screening panel.

"Inside the gate this time?" Setia asked, flinching at the sudden sunlight pouring over them.

"She may as well know I'm a criminal, too," Varric grumbled, but he didn't mean it. He assumed Bernadea would think they hopped the fence rather than think he was an Interloper. Kid Interlopers didn't exist, after all.

They entered her house through the automatic sliding doors.

"Bernadea?" Setia called.

As they passed through the doorway into the main area of the home, the Waveling in the crystal thrashed and clawed at

Varric, like always. He was tired of being treated like garbage, so he jumped at the crystal and roared at the Waveling. The beast didn't flinch, but it stopped having a tantrum and stared at him.

"Not fun, is it?" he muttered.

"Who's there?" Bernadea shouted from a different room. As usual, she sounded out of breath. Then she jogged into the room—and kept jogging in place as she spoke to them. "How did you get through my gate? Never mind. I don't care. What took you so long to get here?"

"It's barely afternoon," Setia said, frowning.

"Did something happen?" Argo asked.

"Oh, something happened." Even as she jogged, Bernadea's eyebrows shot up and her eyes bugged out. "Everything you told me to find is real! And it's huge! Realm-ending huge!"

"What do you mean?" Varric asked.

"What I mean," Bernadea said, ceasing her jogging and wiping sweat off her forehead with a towel she pulled from her belt, "is that if that Wasteling finds the Wind Sage before you do, our realms are as good as dead."

Chapter 12

Horus and Arakaros

"What?" Varric asked, too stupefied to say anything else. His heart leaped into his throat and threatened to strangle him. "You're kidding, right?"

"Not at all." Bernadea flapped a hand in front of her face to cool herself as she tucked her towel back into her belt. "It took a while to dig up the information. Once I knew where to dig, it was all there. Everything you're looking for originates from the Fracturing."

"That long ago?" Setia asked.

"What's the Fracturing?" Varric flinched as they all looked at him in surprise. "What?"

"It's only the single most important event in our history," Setia said. "You really don't know?"

"I really don't know." Varric shuffled in place and ruffled his hood around his head to cover his burning cheeks. He hadn't had the greatest education growing up, so it wasn't his fault.

Argo tousled Varric's hair. "The Fracturing happened over a thousand years ago. It's what created our realms."

"Our realms were created?"

"Yes. By the King of Realms," Bernadea said, earning Varric's undivided attention. "Originally, only two realms existed: Sowengard for the humans and Radomere for the beasts. The beasts were originally called Ethari, by the way. Around the time of the Fracturing, humans stopped using the word." She plopped down on her swivel chair at her tech device and pressed some buttons, bringing up words on the panel. "Back then, the two realms shared something called the Rainbow Path, a river of colors across the sky that represented the movement of magic between our realms. Our realms were two parts of one whole, sharing magic and coexisting. Humans and Ethari got along well enough at the time."

"It didn't stay that way." Setia's hands curled into fists. "The beasts attacked us and stole our magic. Humans created Orbeels in an attempt to hide our magic from the beasts. But the beasts still took so much magic from us that Sowengard itself began to collapse. So we humans went to war against them. As if trying to steal our magic and make our realm crumble weren't bad enough, they summoned their most powerful beast to destroy us."

"Arakaros," Argo said to Varric. "Arakaros would probably make those Crablings in Clobalt look like cuddly pets."

"That bad?" Varric asked.

"Worse." Setia huffed. "He was so powerful he nearly tore apart our realm. Especially after he and the other beasts stole all our magic."

"Then the King of Realms arrived." Bernadea swiveled away from her buttons and faced Varric, adjusting her glasses on her nose. The light from the panel flashed off her lenses. "The King of Realms was the most powerful magic-using human in history. His name was Horus. He singlehandedly faced off against Arakaros and banished him into a separate realm he created."

"The King of Realms created a realm?" Varric stepped forward, his heart fluttering. He couldn't believe he'd never heard any of that before.

"He's not the King of Realms for no reason," Bernadea said, chuckling. She kicked her short legs over the edge of the chair. "The King of Realms is capable of creating, reshaping, and destroying any and all realms. Or so the stories go."

"Arakaros tried to destroy our realms, but Horus saved us by fracturing Sowengard," Setia explained. "The single realm broke into the hundreds of different realms we have today."

"Horus cast Arakaros into a realm called Feldavar and saved our human realms from destruction," Bernadea said.

"He threw all the remaining beasts back into Radomere and blocked them from returning to our realms, too." Setia smiled and her eyes twinkled. Varric had never seen her so passionate about something. "Horus created the systems we use today that guard and protect against beasts hopping between realms."

"With especially strong defenses between Radomere and the human realms," Bernadea added. "Most beasts in Radomere can't return here."

"Why are there still beasts in our realms, then?" Varric hooked a thumb toward the Waveling in the crystal.

"Horus wasn't cruel. He let the beasts remain who didn't threaten humans," Setia said.

The Waveling thrashed in its crystal, hitting the sides so hard the crystal wobbled on its pedestal.

"Don't act like a victim, Waveling," Bernadea muttered. "Or did you forget about trying to drown Iloria City?"

Bernadea huffed at the Waveling, and the Waveling stopped flailing and huffed right back.

"My dagger and Argo's ax do what Horus did. Our weapons throw beasts back into Radomere and trap them there," Varric said.

"Powerful magic. And rare," Bernadea said, nodding. "The ability to cross realms is increasingly uncommon. Even Interlopers have become rare, the sneaky scoundrels. Pity, because I'd love to study them."

A shiver swept over Varric at the sudden deranged look in her eyes. He gulped and hoped he didn't look too guilty. He didn't feel like being someone's experiment.

"So Arakaros is still stuck in Feldavar?" he asked. "Can the beasts go there and help him?"

"That's where Iloria's relic, the Wasteling thief, and Khalkar come in. The details are lacking, so I'm guessing this wasn't common knowledge, even back then." Bernadea swiveled back to her buttons and poked them at high speeds. Reflected letters flowed across her glasses. "The King of Realms banished Arakaros because Arakaros couldn't be destroyed. Instead, Horus attempted to lock Feldavar and make it inaccessible to humans and Ethari. He captured three of the most powerful Ethari called the Sages and used their powers to create boundaries around Feldavar that can't be breached. To destroy the boundaries, one must gather the Sages."

"And then Horus destroyed the Sages so they couldn't be gathered, right?" Setia asked, sounding hopeful.

"Wrong. Like Arakaros, the Sages can't be destroyed. Their bodies can be ruined, but their magic is always inherited by another. Instead, Horus focused on imprisoning them as well. He trapped them in their own realms."

"Let me guess. Khalkar is one of those realms." Argo tapped the toe of one boot on the floor.

"Absolutely," Bernadea declared. "It's the only one I found. I know little else about them. I do know that each Sage is locked inside a special gate, and each gate is sealed by a magical relic."

"Iloria's relic?" Setia placed her hands over her mouth. Her brow creased and her eyes crinkled in grief. "It opens something that powerful?"

"Things get worse," Bernadea said, sounding a little too excited about sharing her bad news. "Once it opens the gate, the relic is destroyed."

"No!" Varric exclaimed. He needed that relic!

"We can't let Iloria's relic be destroyed," Setia agreed, equally as passionate.

"If the Sage is released," Argo asked, "what happens?"

"The Sages are Ethari of unimaginable magical powers. If they get free, they'll change the condition of our realms in ways that would be lethal to humans." Bernadea's brow furrowed. "In the little info I found, it's noted that the Sages didn't help Horus willingly. They sided with Arakaros in his efforts to destroy humanity. If freed, they would use their powers against us."

"If they're anything like Arakaros," Argo said, "their release isn't something we can risk. Arakaros almost obliterated all of Sowengard before the Fracturing." He stood stiffly and clenched his jaw, but he seemed to be taking the news better than Varric and Setia. "What could a fraction of that power do against our smaller realms?"

"Do you think the beasts want to free Arakaros?" Setia asked, glancing between Argo and Bernadea. "Or just release the Sages to hurt humans?"

"If I were an Ethari, I'd want Arakaros back," Argo said. "Humans can stop the Sages. We can't stop Arakaros."

"This is all conjecture for now." Bernadea took out her towel and wiped her head, as if talking was making her sweaty. "But let's assume the Ethari want to release Arakaros. In order to do that, the three Sages need to be released and their powers combined. The only one capable of doing that is the King of Realms. My guess is that if they go after the Sages, they'll try to find the King, too."

"Does anyone even know who the King of Realms is now?" Setia frowned. "I thought he and his family died years ago."

"Yes, but his magic is inheritable for all eternity," Bernadea said. "It's a type of magic that passes through the family line of Horus. Like Arakaros and the Sages, the magic can't be destroyed. If the current King dies, the power leaps to the closest heir."

"But if they all die?" Setia asked.

"It would keep passing on to the next closest blood relative." Bernadea tossed her sweat rag onto the table. "The previous King of Realms was king of modern Sowengard, prior to its destruction. His entire family perished, so we don't know who inherited his magic. Someone in his distant family and distant bloodline must have inherited them without realizing it."

"And you think the beasts will start looking for that person?" Setia asked.

"Without a doubt, if their target is Arakaros. The King of Realms is their only way into Feldavar."

"What if the people who inherit the magic of the King of Realms never realize they have it?" Setia pressed.

"It's hard to say," Bernadea admitted. "The royal line of Sowengard always inherited the magic within the immediate family, and theirs was a closely guarded secret. Outsiders know about the King of Realms and his exceptional magic, but we don't know much about how it all works."

"Regardless, for right now, we can't let the Ethari use Iloria's relic to release the Sage." Argo turned toward Varric, making

Varric jump at the sudden focus. "If that happens, there's nothing you can return to King Garthro."

"King Garthro?" Varric tilted his head to the side.

"Setia's father, the king of Iloria."

"Oh." Varric's face burned. Compared to the others, he didn't know anything.

He ran his hands down his face. His brain was overloaded with new information. It was a lot to process. He was worried about the explosive bracelet and earning his freedom, but that didn't matter as much anymore. All he could think about was how his realm had crumbled and been destroyed. He remembered the screams of the people as they tried to escape. He remembered his mom screaming for him to save her. When he'd tried, he'd failed. Grief welled up in his chest. He'd never wish that suffering on anyone, not even his worst enemies.

"The relic is important, but what really matters is stopping them from releasing the Sage," he stated. "If they can destroy realms, or even really mess up a realm, we can't let that happen."

"Agreed," Setia said. "But how can we reach Khalkar and ensure the Wasteling doesn't release the Sage? There's no way in."

"No known way. But a magical way, perhaps." Bernadea grabbed her exercise bars—the little ones she called dumbbells—and began curling them below the chair and over her head. "Ethari might know magical ways in."

"Maybe the Ethari could help us?" Varric suggested, but Bernadea and Setia looked at him like he was crazy.

"Do you know about something called the Blushing Pond?" Argo asked Bernadea.

"Now you're talking my language, big boy." She dropped her weights to the floor and swiveled around, pushing her buttons. "That one's easy. It's a myth, or so they say."

"Explain."

"Apparently, anyone who finds the Blushing Pond is granted a certain wish. The problem is that no one has ever found it, of course."

"It's not real?" Setia's shoulders sank.

"If it is, it's too hard to reach." Bernadea's fingers flew over the buttons, and letters scrawled over her tech panel. "A method of reaching the pond was written centuries ago. And I quote, 'One must find a Mindling and mind their way through the Forest of Reflections. The brave of heart shall fall into thyself. The one who finds the Blushing Pond will find their way at dawn.'"

"Why is that so hard to find?" Varric asked. "What's the Forest of Reflections?"

"It's here in Iloria. The hard part is the Mindling," Setia said.

"What's a Mindling?"

"Boy, do you know anything?" Bernadea broke into a fit of laughter before collecting her dumbbells and resuming her arm curls. "Mindlings are mythological Ethari. We only know of them through myths like the Blushing Pond. Supposedly, they can read the hearts and minds of humans, distinguishing good from evil. They can hear the minds of men from miles away and flee from them, never to be seen."

"So that probably won't help us find a way to Khalkar." Setia sighed and rubbed her forehead.

"What if it does?" Argo asked. Everyone turned to him with bewildered looks. "What? Knoll suggested we look into it. He was right about everything else. We only need a Mindling."

"Only need!" Bernadea snorted.

"Mindlings are just a myth." Setia pinched the bridge of her nose.

"Are they?" Argo grinned from ear to ear. "We should ask the Mindling I bonded with if he's a myth or not."

Chapter 13

A Cute Little Puffball

Bernadea dropped her weights, her arms still up in a partial curl. Varric and Setia gaped at Argo, who had his hands on his hips and wore his smuggest smile.

"You bonded with a Mindling?" Setia laughed awkwardly, turned straight faced and serious, and then laughed again. "You're lying."

"Show us!" Varric exclaimed, grabbing Argo's arm in both hands and jumping up and down. Mythological beasts sounded awesome! He imagined a giant raging beast with fangs as big as Bernadea's house. "I want to see! Show us!"

Argo patted Varric on the head and then held out his hand. "Come, Frodis."

Light flashed over his palm, and a creature appeared that fit in his hand. It emitted a faint light from its whole body, and it had big round eyes that shone like the twin moons. Feathers protruded from its head. Its body was round, fluffy, and white, and it had iridescent wings. It wrapped its long tail around Argo's wrist as it stood on its stumpy hind legs to get a good look around. Its front paws curled close to its body. It wasn't what Varric had expected, but looking at it made him feel warm and fuzzy.

"Impossible." Bernadea slid from her chair. She adjusted her lenses repeatedly, never blinking.

"It's cute. Can I hold it?" Varric scooted closer and held out his hand.

Unlike all the other beasts that hated Varric, Frodis's eyes brightened at the sight of him. The critter's tail lashed wildly. Frodis chirped and lunged into Varric's outstretched hand, wrapping its tail around his wrist. Warmth and happiness bubbled up in Varric. His heart swelled with joy in a way he couldn't remember feeling before. A smile broke out on his lips, and he cuddled the critter to his cheek. Frodis nuzzled against him in return.

"Impressive," Argo said. "Frodis rarely likes people."

"It's fluffy." Varric giggled as Frodis rubbed its head against his jaw.

"He's male, by the way," Argo said.

"You named it Frodis?" Setia asked, raising an eyebrow.

"Most Ethari already have names, same as humans," Argo said.

"I'll admit it's a rare specimen I've never heard described before, nonetheless seen." Bernadea adjusted her glasses for the billionth time. "But how do you know this is a Mindling?"

"I know a Minder, the human equivalent of a Mindling. Less powerful, but the magic is similar. The Minder informed me Frodis is legitimate. But that's not the only thing. Frodis can read minds and shares with me what he perceives."

Varric froze, staring first in horror at Argo and then at the little creature in his hands. He had a lot of things in his mind that he didn't want anyone to know. What could the creature see? Things he was thinking about? His memories? He had to distract himself! Hide his thoughts! Giant monsters with fangs as big as Bernadea's house! Sweet berry candies shaped like kittens! Endless meat buns falling from the clouds! His stomach grumbled as he handed Frodis back to Argo.

Varric cleared his throat. "R-read minds?"

"Don't worry. It's not as creepy as you're thinking." Argo chuckled. "Frodis might be able to understand what you're thinking, but he can't clearly communicate that information with me. It's rare for Ethari to speak the human language, even if they understand us." Argo tickled the top of Frodis's head, eyeing Varric. "Right now, Frodis is communicating that you're trying to hide your thoughts from him. Bernadea is trying to overcome the desire to trap and study him. And Setia . . ." Argo paused, and his smile softened. "She's trying to hide thoughts, too. Images in people's minds are easier for Frodis to transmit to me. Emotions pass along well, too."

"What am I thinking right now?" Varric asked, imagining a cloud shaped like a butterfly.

Argo grinned. "A cloud shaped like a butterfly." Varric thought about something else. Argo raised an eyebrow. "Now a cat riding a donkey. What's wrong with you?" Then Varric imagined Bernadea weightlifting Argo over her head. Argo chuckled and shook his head. "I'm not saying that out loud."

"I think he's telling the truth," Varric said, laughing.

"Frodis can do more than that." Argo went to the Waveling in the crystal, holding out Frodis on his hand. "Frodis, can you tell me about this Waveling?"

Frodis sat on his hindquarters and inspected the crystal. He chirped and chattered at the Waveling, who stared at him in surprise. Then the Waveling swished back and forth in the crystal, its lips moving, but it didn't make a sound.

"This Waveling is named Preena," Argo said. "She's actually quite brave. Many Wavelings intended to attack Iloria City that day, but she was the only one who went through with it."

"Why did they attack?" Bernadea asked.

"Hatred. That's all Frodis senses and shares with me, at least." Argo drew Frodis back to himself. "That's common among Ethari, to be honest. Most Ethari hate humans because we defeated Arakaros and trapped many of them in Radomere."

"Shouldn't they be happy that some of them got to stay here?" Varric asked.

Preena thrashed against the crystal walls, bouncing back and forth. When she stopped, she glared and showed her fangs to Varric.

"Her rage suggests she disagrees," Argo said.

"Never did I think I'd see a Mindling . . . a living myth." Bernadea flopped into her chair and resumed curling her dumbbells. Still, her eyes remained stuck on Frodis.

"Argo apparently has all sorts of legendary Ethari up his sleeve." Varric grinned.

"Can Frodis check and see if we're all . . . trustworthy?" Setia asked.

Varric glared at her. Who else could she be talking about besides him? Sure, he'd tried to steal the relic, but he hadn't done anything else. He hadn't even tried to steal gold from Argo. Just because he looked like a thief didn't mean she had to assume he was the worst person in the realms.

"Since Frodis came when summoned, I already know the answer," Argo said. "Frodis won't appear if there are humans around who have evil in their hearts."

"Sometimes you can't summon him?" Setia continually looked stunned.

"I'm bonded to my companion Ethari. They aren't my slaves. If they don't want to show up, they won't come when I call them."

"Has that happened before?"

"Only with Frodis and only around certain people."

"What do the Ethari get out of the deal?" Varric asked. "Why would they bond with a human?"

"Depends on the Ethari," Argo said. "Most Ethari unite with Bonders because it gives them some sort of security. Since humans rule the realms, it helps Ethari to be companionable to them."

"And your companions?"

"I saved Frodis, and that impressed him. He joined me as thanks for saving him." Argo held out Frodis, and the little Ethari leaped back into Varric's hands. Varric cuddled the creature, appreciating the fluffy feelings that filled his chest. Argo continued, "Novi could only be reached by someone pure of heart. I brought Frodis with me to meet her, proving my worth. She joined me out of curiosity. As for Cerbrus, I challenged him to a duel. I survived longer than he expected. Now he joins me because he enjoys partaking in battles with strong opponents. And then there's—"

"Novi and Cerbrus?" Bernadea had stopped mid-curl, her eyes frozen on Argo. "The legendary beasts? More myths?"

"Go big or go home." Argo grinned.

"You said, 'And then,'" Setia said, her brow furrowing. "Do you have *another* companion?"

"Wouldn't you like to know?" Argo winked and scooped Frodis into his hand. "I'm starting to get a headache, so it's probably time for you to go. Thanks for the visit, pal." He bopped Frodis on the head with his thumb and sent him away.

"What sort of power do you think I'd gain if I copied Frodis's abilities?" Setia wondered.

"Not sure. But he didn't want you to touch him," Argo said with a shrug. "He knows you're a Shifter."

Setia's face crumpled in disappointment.

Varric grinned, finally feeling vindicated, at least a little. "But he let the smelly boy touch him." For good measure, he stuck out his tongue at Setia. "So what now? Are we going to the Blushing Pond?"

"The Forest of Reflections is several days from here. We don't have a lot of time to waste." Setia folded her arms and rubbed them. "Are we going to trust Knoll and risk going that far? What if he's lying?"

"He hasn't lied yet," Varric pointed out.

"We don't have a lot of time to risk losing." She eyed the bracelet on his wrist. "It's already been five days. You only have two weeks, Varric. Going to the Forest of Reflections will take days. That doesn't leave a lot of wiggle room."

Varric rubbed the explosive bracelet. "If the Blushing Pond really does grant a wish, maybe we can just wish the relic back into our possession. We don't have any other leads, do we?"

"Bernadea, can you run that Wasteling's information again and see if it left Clobalt?" Argo asked.

"Hmm . . ." Bernadea set her dumbbells on the table and turned to her board of buttons. Her fingers flew over them at high speeds, bringing up letters on her panel. "It looks like it departed Clobalt shortly after you went to retrieve it." Her eyes squinted, and she scrunched her lips from side to side. "It went to a few other known realms and eventually vanished."

"To Khalkar?" Setia leaned toward the panel to inspect it, earning a sideways glare from Bernadea.

"Perhaps. Or to any other realm that doesn't allow Pellios to use their tracking system."

"So we have no other leads," Varric said.

"We could always go back and ask Knoll for more information," Setia suggested.

"I think he told us all that he wanted to tell us. He's the one who told us about the Blushing Pond, remember?"

"I don't want to go so far astray only to learn there's nothing there. We don't have much time." Setia took a step toward him. "You don't have much time, Varric." Real, genuine concern showed on her face and in her eyes. When Varric didn't respond, she turned toward Argo. "Help me with this. Surely you see the flaws in chasing a myth."

Argo stood with one hand on his hip and the other hand scratching his scruffy facial hair. His intense focus stayed on Varric. "I want that bracelet off you," he admitted, and Varric's heartbeat stuttered at the obvious concern. "I also know that myths can be real if we know where to look for them."

"Argo—" Setia began to argue, but he held up a hand to stop her.

"We still have a little time," he said. "If we find nothing at the Blushing Pond, we can go back to Knoll and ask for more information."

"Or maybe the Wasteling will show up again in Bernadea's tech and we can chase him. But for now, this is all we have." Varric waved his explosive bracelet in the air. "I'm the one who's going to explode, remember? And I think this is the best thing we can do right now."

"If you say so . . ." Setia stood straight, and her former indecision vanished. "If this is your decision, I'll follow you and do what I can to help."

Varric nodded, unsure of what to say.

"Bernadea, is there anything else you can tell us about the Blushing Pond?" Argo asked.

"Nothing besides the myth I told you," she said, repeating the myth for them.

"Do you know how to get to the Forest of Reflections?" Varric asked Setia.

"Yes. It's several days from here."

"We'll want to grab some supplies in Iloria City before we go," Argo suggested.

"Then let's stop wasting time and get moving. We have a lot of ground to cover." Varric slammed his fist into his open palm. He made for the door, waving over his shoulder at Bernadea. "Thanks for the help, Bernie!"

Bernadea scowled at him as they departed.

Chapter 14

An Army of Sticks

After stopping in Iloria City to buy supplies, Varric and the others set off for the Forest of Reflections. Their journey brought them over rolling hills and through fertile valleys. Plants of all varieties thrived throughout the realm. Winglings frolicked in the air with the birds. Wavelings floated through rivers and lakes. Iloria was full of life.

They camped several times along the way, taking turns keeping watch at night. Thankfully, they didn't come across anything dangerous. Part of Varric wanted to see Argo use his super cool Ethari to fight again, but they didn't have time to waste.

Finally, they reached a forest that sprawled across the horizon. By then, all the roads and trails had been overrun by plant life. Few humans traveled that far. The forest looked like any other forest in Iloria, with massively tall trees and thick canopies. Setia led them through a curtain of vines speckled with little white flowers and into the shadows of the trees.

"Do we need to use Frodis now?" Varric asked, but Setia shook her head.

"We're not at the Forest of Reflections yet. Just wait."

They ventured deeper into the forest. Setia pushed past several more flowering curtains and stepped into an area with fewer trees but dozens of pools of water. The trees had sparse branches that let in bright streaks of sunlight, giving the area a shining, magical feel. Little flecks of dust or pollen floated in the sunbeams.

"Ponds?" Varric stopped beside Setia. He'd been expecting more trees and less water, especially looking for a place with *forest* in the name. Then again, all the ponds had glass-like surfaces, making them perfect for reflections.

"Quiet," Setia whispered. "This place is considered sacred by the people of Iloria. Some people come here to devote themselves to silence and solitude. They usually come back enlightened."

"Usually?" Varric echoed.

"Some don't come back at all."

"So maybe they did find the Blushing Pond?"

"Or died trying." Argo grinned when Varric and Setia glared at him. He held out his hand. "Frodis, come." The little Ethari appeared on his palm, eyeing Argo expectantly. "We're looking for the Blushing Pond. Can you help us?"

Frodis stood on his hind legs and took in his surroundings. His head feathers fluttered. Chirping, he burst off Argo's hand and zipped away.

"I take that as a yes," Varric said.

Argo led the way, barely jogging to keep Frodis's pace. Setia didn't seem to have trouble keeping up with them, but Varric was in a full-on sprint and still lagging behind. As they passed one pond, he happened to glance down. Instead of seeing a reflection of him running like a lunatic, he saw himself dangling upside down from a branch over the heads of Ilorian guards, right before he'd tried to steal the relic. The reflection made him trip on his own feet. Glancing at the next nearest pond, he saw himself crawling on his belly through some underbrush, spying on Iloria's castle while planning his theft. These definitely weren't ordinary reflections.

"Look! I see my memories in the water," Varric shouted at his allies, who had moved on without him. Argo and Setia returned. Frodis eventually came back, fluttering over Argo's head.

"I see my memories, too." Setia leaned over the pond before moving to another. Her gaze drifted around the forest.

"I see mine," Argo said. "Powerful magic is at work here." He stared at the water before his gaze drifted to Varric. Pain flashed across his eyes, but he hastily turned away. "Let's keep moving. Don't get distracted."

Setia hesitantly followed, but she looked at the ponds at every opportunity. Varric crouched and splashed the water. The reflection rippled but didn't change. He looked at the distant ponds and saw only ordinary reflections. The water must only show memories when a person got close.

Varric sprinted after Argo and Setia, catching glimpses of ponds and memories as he passed. He saw his mom sitting in her usual chair, her vacant eyes staring into nothingness. He saw his sisters kneeling beside their mom's bed, sobbing for her to be well again. He saw his mom screaming for him to do something as their realm collapsed. He saw her drop to the floor, injured because he didn't save her. Agonizing grief tore through his chest and brought stinging tears to his eyes. He refused to look at the water anymore. Instead, he focused his thoughts on when he might eat the leftover food in his pouch, distracting himself so Frodis wouldn't share any private information with Argo.

Some rustling in the nearby trees slowed his steps. Branches came alive, twisting and turning—and revealing faces with beady black eyes.

Varric let out a bewildered shout and pointed. "Look!"

Once again, Argo and Setia stopped at his call. Strange beasts dropped out of the sparse trees and gathered on the edges of the woods that surrounded the Forest of Reflections. They had bodies like thick sticks and six legs that looked like branches, plus two arms that looked like extra-long twigs. Leaves of all varieties sprouted from different joints all over their bodies.

"Treelings!" Varric exclaimed.

"Those are Leaflings." Setia shook her head. "You can't just name things whatever you want."

"They look more like trees than leaves. Branchlings. Twiglings."

"Stop."

Rustling from behind made Varric and Setia turn. Both shouted in alarm when a small army of Leaflings scurried up to them. They backed into Argo, who pulled them away from the crowding Ethari.

"Are they trapping us?" Varric asked.

"Herding us, maybe. Leading us somewhere?" Setia rubbed the Orbeel on her bracer.

"We're not interested in a fight. Please let us pass in peace," Argo called to the Leaflings. The Leaflings ceased their advance.

Frodis returned for them, squeaking and chirping. Argo followed as the Mindling buzzed forward. Setia and Varric followed. Setia kept Varric ahead of her, probably to keep him from stopping again—which was fine, because she had a weapon and he didn't. He'd let her be closer to the Leaflings. Behind them, the forest came alive with the sounds of rustling branches, whispering leaves, snapping twigs, and tiny footsteps. Varric could only imagine all the Leaflings chasing them, but he didn't look back.

Finally, Frodis circled a pool. It looked like all the others and was in the middle of the pond forest. Scattered trees cast it in shadows, but a few sunbeams dappled its surface. Varric, Argo, and Setia stood in the grass by the pool and looked around as the clattering sounds of the forest came to an abrupt halt. Hundreds of Leaflings had them surrounded. Some of the Leaflings held twigs in their stick arms. Others cluttered the branches of nearby trees and peered at them through the foliage. Varric and Setia stepped a little closer to Argo.

"Are they gonna fight us?" Varric asked. He glanced down at the pond Frodis found for them. A sinking feeling settled in his gut. "This pond's reflection is normal."

"Great. We found the one normal pond. Now what?" Setia muttered, pressing her back to Argo's side so the Leaflings couldn't sneak up on her. Varric did the same.

"Frodis hears a voice from the pond. I can't understand it," Argo said.

"A voice from the pond?" Varric felt awkward with the hundreds of beady eyes staring at them.

"What did the myth say?" Setia asked. "After the Mindling. What next?"

"The brave of heart shall fall into thyself," Argo said.

"What does that mean?" Varric scooted further behind Argo when the Leaflings clustered closer.

"Maybe it means we need to jump in the water that shows our reflection?" Setia suggested. "Since this is the only pool that literally reflects our images back at us?"

That made sense. Why else would this pond be the only one that showed their reflection like a mirror? Plus, Frodis picked it.

Varric sat in the grass on the edge of the pool and slid in, feet first. He cried out in surprise when the water didn't catch him and he fell straight through like it wasn't even there. Over the sudden rush of wind, he heard Setia and Argo shouting after him. Then their voices silenced.

The forest vanished in a blink, replaced by a reddish-orange sky. Varric flailed his arms and legs in open air, and then he splashed into water. Bubbles frothed around him, tangling his arms and legs in his cloak. He thrashed and struggled, keeping his eyes on the orange coloring he knew would take him to the surface. As he turned vertical, his boots brushed solid ground. He pushed off and sprang to the surface, taking in a gulp of air.

Frodis swooped near his head. A moment later, Argo and Setia appeared out of a portal in the air and plummeted into the water. When they surfaced, they both sputtered.

"When I made the suggestion, I didn't mean for you to hop right in," Setia said, blowing water off her lips and brushing her ponytail away from her face. "Maybe throw a stick in first? What if it was dangerous?"

"Too late now. It was some kind of portal. I saw it when you guys fell through." Varric looked upward, but the portal had disappeared.

He paddled his way to the edge of the pool. The pool itself was about three times bigger than the pools in the Forest of Reflections. A sandy beach surrounded it, and the beach was surrounded by big rocks. Varric dragged himself out of the deep water and onto the beach. When he stood, he saw a lush forest, a vibrant sunset, and—he stopped. Argo and Setia joined him and followed his gaze toward a large pool of water set among rocks in the midst of the trees. The surface of the pool was as still as glass and perfectly pink. Not orange like the sunset, not tinted from the colored sky, but totally pink.

"That is a very pink pond," Varric said.

Setia gaped at it. "The Blushing Pond is real."

"Argo is our lucky charm. He makes myths real." Varric grinned at their big companion. Even Argo stared at the pink water like he couldn't believe what he saw. Frodis had landed on his shoulder.

"Let's hope having a wish granted is real, too." Argo ran his fingers through his hair and climbed over the rocks toward the pond.

Varric and Setia scrambled after him. Varric was a little less graceful because his wet cloak weighed him down and his smaller legs made the tall rocks hard to navigate. As they approached the pink pond, he didn't hear anything besides their steps on the rocks. No breeze, no creatures. Nothing.

"Why is it so late here? It was barely mid-morning in the Forest of Reflections," Setia said as she inspected the sunset sky. Her gaze drifted to their immediate surroundings, her face tightening. "I don't hear anything here. Where are we?"

"Some sort of realm where time stopped, perhaps?" Argo stepped to the rocky edge of the Blushing Pond.

"Is that possible?" Varric asked.

"I've heard of realms like that existing, but I've never been to one."

They gathered at the edge of the pond and looked expectantly into the water, but nothing happened. It showed their reflection like any other pool, even though it was pink. Looking straight down, the water was clear, with only a pinkish tinge, and it was only a couple of inches deep. The bottom was covered in pearly white pebbles. Varric reached for the water, but Setia grabbed his arm in both hands.

"Don't! What if it's dangerous?" She jerked her head toward the nearby trees. "Touch it with a stick first."

Varric rolled his eyes and touched the water.

"Varric!"

"Nothing happened," he said to appease her, shrugging. He stepped back from the water, a little disappointed. "Now what?"

"Bernadea's myth said we'd find our way at dawn." Argo crossed his arms and looked at the sun, which sank toward the horizon. The orange sky faded into purple. "The sun appears to be setting, so we'll have to wait."

"We could always teleport back to Iloria City for a bite to eat," Varric said hopefully. After their trip to the Forest of Reflections, they'd used most of their fresh provisions. He still had a loaf of bread and some jerky, but he wanted to save them for an emergency.

"That works for me. Though I wonder if we'll be able to teleport straight back here." Argo scratched his facial scruff.

"Let's try. Hopefully we can come right back." Varric teleported—but didn't.

Nothing happened. He felt no trace of his magic. His heart stuttered as his friends looked at him. His throat tightened.

"I can't use my magic," he squeaked.

Chapter 15

Trees Don't Talk

"Now that you mention it . . ." Argo held Frodis on his palm and frowned. "I don't have a headache from keeping Frodis out for so long. I can't connect with his mind, either."

Setia closed her eyes and then popped them open. "I can't access my powers, either." Turning in a circle, she examined their surroundings with her lips pressed tight. Fear flashed through her eyes. "This realm is blocking our magic. We're trapped."

"Until dawn, at least," Argo said, keeping calm despite the fear pinching Varric and Setia's voices. He set Frodis on his shoulder. "Let's get settled here and build a fire. When dawn arrives, we'll see what happens. Shall we?"

"Fine. Let's look for something to eat." Setia rubbed her upper arms and glanced around. "If there's anything alive out there. How can the trees be so quiet?"

"Trees don't talk, Setia," Varric said, throwing in an eye roll. "Those were Treelings chasing us in the forest, remember? Not real trees."

"I meant animals in the trees. Insects." Setia dropped her arms to her sides and glared at him.

"So you don't deny that they were Treelings instead of Leaflings?"

"Go find food." Huffing, Setia stormed off into the trees.

Argo chuckled and wandered off in another direction. Varric grinned as he went a different way, heading toward the sunset. He searched the trees for fruit, looked for edible berries and flowers, and even hunted for any signs of animals. He didn't find anything. Besides trees, grass, and weeds, the place was barren. He only walked a short distance before he reached the glaring white wall at the edge of the realm. The sun set behind it.

Sighing, he marched back to the Blushing Pond. It didn't take long for his allies to return—empty-handed, just like him. By the time they came back together, it was dark, with stars sprinkling the sky. It had gotten dark unnaturally fast. At least they could see. The Blushing Pond radiated a dull pink light. Frodis radiated light, too.

"How is there nothing here?" Setia muttered after they exchanged reports.

"The realm ends abruptly. It's a pretty small place." Argo eyed the sky, scratching his chin. "Time is moving strangely here. I expect dawn will arrive sooner than we think. Let's make a fire and get comfortable."

Argo built a fire near the Blushing Pond while Varric and Setia gathered wood. They also cleared the area so they had space to lie down. At least it was warm, so they didn't need blankets. Varric's cloak would keep him plenty comfortable.

Still, Varric hated feeling trapped. He depended on his magic to find food and to escape from danger. If something awful happened now, like a giant monster attacking, he wouldn't be able to escape. It made him feel even worse because it was the only skill he had to offer his allies, and now it was gone.

As they settled down by the fire, Frodis fluttered from Argo to Varric, crawling inside his cloak, climbing up his chest, and poking his head out his neck hole. Varric laughed and nuzzled against the fuzzy creature, feeling warmer and safer with him there. Setia squinted at them in envy.

Varric's stomach rumbled, so he pulled out his leftover food. The bread was a little soggy on the outside but still edible. His instincts told him to save some food for later, but if he split it, they could each have a little something to eat to get through the night.

"Here." He broke up the pieces into equal portions and gave some to Argo and Setia.

"Thank you." Setia took hers and plopped down with her back to a rock, crisscrossing her legs in front of her.

"Thanks." Argo received his with a warm smile. He sat farthest from the fire, his long legs stretched in front of him, his back to a log.

Varric sat in a patch of grass closest to the fire. His clothes had almost dried, but he still felt chilly. They ate in relative silence, with only the crackling fire and their subtle movements providing any sound. His mind wandered to thoughts of his mom and sisters. He hoped they were okay. Were his sisters worried about him? He'd told them he'd be back soon. Did Jonavad wonder if he'd been imprisoned or killed? Would he come after him somehow? Varric doubted it. Jonavad always made it clear that Varric was on his own. Varric's thoughts wandered back to the day his realm collapsed. The screams echoed in his mind. He snuggled Frodis, squeezed his eyes shut, and pushed the thoughts away.

"Varric," Setia hesitantly said. She drew her legs to her chest and wrapped her arms around them. "I know I asked you before, but the longer we're together, the more important it seems." Shifting uncomfortably, she met his eyes. "Why did you try to steal the relic?"

Varric nestled further into his cloak, heat rushing to his cheeks. She hadn't been that forward about it since they'd first left Iloria. Now she seemed more concerned than angry. Varric stared at the fire, because he couldn't look at the sympathy in her eyes. Not many people looked at him like that. No one, in fact. Maybe only her and Argo.

Should he tell them the truth? Would it hurt anything? Jonavad always warned him to keep his family a secret. He reminded Varric that everyone would hate him for what happened. But it probably wouldn't hurt to mention his mom. They had to assume he had a mom, right? He didn't have to share details. Would Setia let him use the relic if he was honest about it and she realized how important it was to him?

After a while, Setia's shoulders sank and she returned her gaze to the flames. Embers leaped through her eyes. Her brow scrunched in disappointment, and guilt wormed through Varric's chest. It shouldn't have bothered him that it bothered her, but it did.

"What about you, Princess?" Argo tossed a stick into the fire. "Why come after the relic yourself when you could just send guards to keep an eye on Varric?"

Setia plucked a stick off the ground and swirled it in the flames, stirring up an explosion of embers. The fire crackled and popped.

"I want to prove my worth to my father," she admitted, tossing the stick into the fire and wrapping her arms around her legs. "For as long as I can remember, nothing I've done has ever satisfied him. Excelling in my studies didn't matter. Neither did my skills as a Shifter or fighter. Finding the relic might actually prove my worth in a way that matters to him."

Varric wasn't sure how to respond to her honesty. He felt bad for her. He didn't clearly remember his parents from early in his childhood. He was young when his realm was destroyed, but he thought he remembered being loved. A sad realization settled over him. He hadn't felt that way since his dad died and his mom was injured. Jonavad looked out for him, but it wasn't the same. It was hard for Varric not having parents to care for him. How much harder was it for Setia to have a dad who intentionally ignored her? He thought about his own mom and the vacant look in her eyes, how she saw right through him. Even though he knew it wasn't her fault, it still hurt him. Is that what Setia felt?

"While we're being honest," Argo said, smiling faintly at Setia before dropping his gaze back to the flames, "I'm looking for my son. He disappeared in an accident some years back. I want to use the relic to look for him. Most everyone believes he's dead, but they never recovered a body. I won't stop looking until I know for sure."

Varric's throat tightened. All that time, he thought Argo was a thug or a mercenary, but instead, he was a dad looking for his kid. No wonder he was so desperate to find the relic.

"I'm sorry," Setia whispered. "Is there anything I can do? Do you want me to assign people to search for him?"

"No. I've done everything that can be done." Argo smiled warmly at Setia. "Thank you, though. I appreciate it."

Silence claimed them again. Varric squirmed under his cloak, aware that he'd been entrusted with their important secrets. For the first time in a long time, he felt like he belonged. Maybe it would be okay to tell some of his secrets, too. Maybe not all of them, but he wanted to tell them that something was wrong and show that he wasn't just a petty thief. He was trying to help someone important to him. Jonavad had warned him repeatedly to keep his mouth shut, but what if—

"I'm trying to save my mom," he blurted out before he had time to talk himself out of it. He squeezed Frodis and burrowed deeper into his cloak, suddenly feeling ashamed. Jonavad would be furious if he found out. Varric hated that, but it felt right to finally say it out loud. "She was hurt. I've done everything I can to make her better, but it isn't working. I was going to use the relic to look for something to save her."

The flames leaped and crackled in the eerie silence. Varric felt the eyes of his allies on him, but he didn't look up.

"Oh, Varric," Setia murmured. "Is there anything I can do to help?"

"Only the relic can help now." Varric buried his face, squishing Frodis in the process. The Ethari didn't seem to mind.

Jonavad had already researched every other possible way to heal Varric's mom. He'd also told Varric the relic wouldn't show him anything useful. Jonavad wanted it for other reasons, like maybe releasing the Sage and using their magic to heal his mom? Varric wasn't sure. But how could he not try using the relic if he was going to steal it anyway?

"I didn't realize. I'm sorry." Setia took in a deep breath and sat straight. "When we find the relic, I'll let you both use it before we return it to Iloria."

"That sort of defeats the purpose of you being here, doesn't it?" Argo smiled lazily. "You told your father you'd keep anyone from using it."

"I know. And I won't lie to him." Setia clenched her jaw and shook her head. "But you're both here. You've done a lot to find the relic. That can't be said of anyone from Iloria, even though it's our treasure."

"You're here, aren't you?" Varric reminded her.

"Yes. Because the relic matters to my realm. But it matters to both of you even more. Come what may, I promise I'll let you use the relic."

"Thanks." Varric smiled, and happy warmth spread all the way to his toes.

He nuzzled against Frodis, who nuzzled right back. It was nice to share at least part of his secret, even if Jonavad would be angry. Maybe Varric would find a way to save his mom and everything would be okay.

"Let's get some rest, shall we? May as well make use of the dark and take some naps. In shifts." Argo flopped down on the grass and folded his arms behind his head. "Varric, take first shift. Setia takes the last shift. Wake me in the middle."

"Why you in the middle?" Setia asked, even though they'd always done it that way. She curled up on the ground, her hands pillowed under her head.

"I like to feel like a sandwich," Argo said.

Setia glared at him, but Varric laughed.

"You two are babies," Argo admitted. "I want you both to sleep for as long as possible, uninterrupted. Sleep is good for babies."

"I'm not a baby," Varric and Setia said in harmony. Their eyes met, and Varric's face burned.

"Anyway, that means you should sleep uninterrupted, Argo." Varric feigned concern, softening his voice and pouting. "You're so old. Losing sleep like that might make you—"

"You stop those words in your mouth right now if you know what's good for you." Argo chucked a lump of tree bark at Varric.

Varric and Setia laughed. Argo and Setia settled down to sleep while Varric cuddled with Frodis, peeked at the stars, and prepared to keep watch.

Chapter 16

Frodis gets Eaten

V arric awoke from dreamless slumber to a big hand jostling his shoulder. It was shaking him pretty good, so he must have been sleeping deeply. He blinked several times so his eyes could adjust to the dim lights. Argo was crouched beside him.

"Time to get up, kiddo. It's almost dawn."

Frodis fluttered out of Varric's cloak to Argo's shoulder as Varric sprawled in the grass, stretching his arms and legs as far as they would go. He rolled into an upright position and rubbed sleep out of his eyes. Frodis and the Blushing Pond emitted light, but the sky also brightened and illuminated their surroundings. Argo stood and crossed his arms, searching the area. Setia roamed around the pond, inspecting it from every direction, before returning to them. Varric stood, and they stared at the pond expectantly.

More and more streaks of light burst from the horizon, consuming the stars and coloring the area gold. The Blushing

Pond glowed brighter in the increasing light. Still, nothing happened.

"Do we need to do something—" Varric started, but the ground rumbled and silenced him.

Nearby trees creaked and groaned as the shaking intensified. Argo grabbed Varric and Setia and hauled them away from the Blushing Pond, pushing them behind him. Water erupted from the center of the pond like a fountain, spraying in every direction and glittering in the sunlight. A massive beast rose from the churning waves. Half a beast, anyway. Some of it stayed below the surface.

It looked like a lizard with smooth skin in pearly shades of pink, purple, and white. A neck frill made of flubbery skin wrapped around its head like a mane. Its eyes glared white. The creature's webbed feet clung to the rocks on the edge of the pond. Its head was as big as a Crabling. Varric imagined its body being super long and definitely too big to fit in a pond that was only a couple of inches deep.

Argo further pushed Varric and Setia behind him as the creature leaned its head forward to inspect them. Frodis flew from Argo's shoulder and hovered in front of the beast. He flitted left and right, chattering at it. The beast jerked forward and snapped its mouth shut around Frodis.

"No!" Varric and the others shouted. They ran forward in unison, with Argo in the lead.

"Frodis!" Argo leaped onto the beast's head, grabbed the edges of its lips, and pulled, his muscles bulging.

Varric grabbed the bottom part of the beast's lips and pulled, letting his weight dangle in the air. Setia grabbed rocks and chucked them at the beast's eyes. The beast snarled at them and shook its head, throwing Argo and Varric off. Then it opened its mouth, and Frodis buzzed out.

"Frodis!" Argo ran and met the Mindling, who landed in his outstretched hands.

Varric and Setia got close enough to confirm that Frodis was all right. The Mindling chirped and squeaked, shaking out his wet fur and fluffing up in size.

"An acceptable reaction," said a rich, female voice from the large Ethari. Her lips and mouth didn't move, but the voice was audible. "Anything less and I would have devoured you."

"This was some sort of test?" Argo pulled Frodis to his chest. The Mindling nuzzled against him.

"I have been testing you since the moment you set foot within the Forest of Reflections," the pearly Ethari said. "Your first test was the Mindling, who confirmed you worthy of my time. The Leaflings were your second test. Had you harmed even a single one, I would have let you fall into a different realm that is far less pleasant. Most humans who wander the Forest of Reflections meet such peril."

"You kill them?" Setia's face contorted in anger and disgust.

"They destroy themselves by their own folly," the Ethari said calmly, without any remorse or sympathy. "Your third test was your time spent within my domain. Most humans who come with companions destroy each other before ever meeting me. One wish is not enough to go around for the many. While you dawdled in my domain, I listened to your words and perceived your true intentions. Had you been any less noble, I would have devoured you at dawn."

"And our fourth test was you trying to eat my Mindling." Argo didn't resist the bitterness in his voice. Fury showed in his narrowed eyes and set jaw. Varric had never seen him so serious. Frodis fluttered to Argo's shoulder, pawed at his jaw, and muttered at him.

"Consider it my assurance, as it is a great risk for Ethari to deal with humans. Trust does not come easily, especially considering whom you brought into my presence," said the pearly Ethari. Varric and the others exchanged confused glances. She continued, "But alas, you have made it this far. Let us see how much longer you survive. I am called Kimarda. Why have you so endangered yourselves by entering my presence?"

"Do you control the flow of time in this realm?" Setia waved at the sky.

"Everything you see is an illusion. Even the sky," Kimarda admitted. "I give all humans who enter here from sunset until dawn to either impress me or destroy themselves."

Varric scrunched his face, feeling bad for Kimarda. Her only visitors were people who wanted to use her. He spent most of his time alone, too. Until he met Argo and Setia, he hadn't spent time with anyone consistently for years.

"You're always here alone," he said. "Doesn't that get lonely?"

"It is sufficient for now."

"For now?"

"Enough." Kimarda snorted, shaking her head, her neck frill flapping. "I have no need of your counsel. Tell me why you dared enter my presence."

"As you may have overheard," Setia started, wavering a little, "we hope to find the relic of Iloria."

"We hope to retrieve the relic and return it to Iloria," Argo hastily amended.

"At present, the relic is in the possession of a Wasteling," Kimarda said, opening her jaws wide in a yawn. The fangs she showed made Varric's skin prickle.

"How do you know that?" he asked.

"You have no access to magic here, but I do. I have communicated with your Mindling and understand your quest. Tell me why I should oppose the Wasteling, my fellow Ethari? Why is your quest nobler than his?"

Setia pulled back her shoulders. "Because the beast wants to release Arakaros—"

"You come to my domain and call my brethren 'beasts?'" Kimarda curled her lips to reveal fangs.

"I-I'm sorry . . ." Setia backed away, her hands held up in surrender.

"Forgive us." Argo stepped ahead of Setia. "We only recently learned the word Ethari. Forgive our ignorance. We mean no disrespect."

"Arakaros is leader of the Ethari." Kimarda snorted. "Why should I not rather allow him to be released?"

"Because Arakaros wants to destroy everyone," Varric said.

"Wants to destroy the humans." Kimarda swung her head toward Varric. "Should that trouble me?"

"Yes."

Argo moved into the space between Varric and Kimarda. "We don't mean—"

"Let him speak," Kimarda snapped. She leaned close to Varric, and he caught a whiff of her breath. It smelled strangely sweet, like citrus fruit. "Perhaps the humans deserve to be destroyed."

"Why?" Varric asked.

"You demand answers from me?" Kimarda jolted into an upright position, her neck frill standing straight up on her head, wide and stiff.

"It's a genuine question. I'm not trying to be rude." Varric shrugged.

Setia took a step closer. "What he means is—"

"Silence." Kimarda hissed and leaned so close Varric could've reached out and touched her. "Tell me. Do you suppose it is right that Arakaros remains sealed for his actions many centuries ago?"

Varric frowned, not having given much thought to Arakaros. He'd only recently learned about him. Arakaros entered the human realms to destroy the humans. He was the aggressor—the villain. As powerful as people believed he was, he needed to stay locked away to protect as many lives as possible.

"If he plans on doing the same things he did before, then yes. He should stay locked up," he said.

"And if he vowed that he would never harm again, would you yourself release him?" Kimarda almost purred.

Varric felt like he was being baited into some sort of trap. Still, he considered the question. Would it be possible for Arakaros to change? Did something anger him in the past that made him attack the humans? Would he feel that same anger toward the humans currently alive? It wouldn't be fair for Arakaros to punish the humans living now because of the actions of humans in the past. But it also wouldn't be fair to keep Arakaros locked away forever if he truly had no ill intentions toward the current humans.

"If I knew beyond a doubt that he wouldn't try to destroy us, yes. I'd let him out." Varric nodded. "We could try to work together."

Kimarda jerked away again, fully upright, her neck frill stiff. "You speak truthfully. Alas, I am unconvinced that you are worthy of my time. I will allow you to depart with your lives, but I grant you no wish."

"Please reconsider," Argo said, and Frodis chattered in agreement.

"We need your help. We have nowhere else to turn," Setia added, clasping her hands together.

"Groveling is unbecoming." Kimarda bared her fangs in a creepy smile. "I give you one last opportunity to convince me. Why should I help you instead of my brethren?"

Varric and the others exchanged glances. Setia shrugged. Argo scratched the back of his head. They had no idea what might motivate Kimarda into helping them. Did they have a compelling argument? Varric wanted to save his mom. Argo wanted to find his son. Setia wanted to earn the approval of her father. Ever since they spoke with Knoll, they also wanted to prevent the release of the Sage, who would hurt the human realms. They wanted to prevent Arakaros from being released, because he would probably kill everyone. That was why their path was right and worth Kimarda's help. Kimarda had tested them for kindness and compassion toward Leaflings, each other, and Frodis. That mattered to her.

"Because we aren't trying to hurt anybody," Varric offered.

Setia's shoulders sank, so she was probably disappointed by his answer. Argo wore an indiscernible expression. Maybe he didn't like the answer, either. Kimarda leaned forward, snorting on Varric and sprinkling him with droplets he hoped were water. Argo extended one hand like he planned on snatching Varric away, but he stopped, and Varric held his ground.

"You are not what I expected," Kimarda said after a long moment of scrutinizing Varric. "A keen argument, but is it your best?"

"Motives matter to you, don't they? You made us come with a Mindling." Varric shrugged, secretly hoping he wasn't making matters worse for them. "Aren't our motives better than most?"

Kimarda tilted her head. The tip of her tongue flicked out of her mouth and tasted the air before slurping back inside. "Very well. I acquiesce to your request."

"Ac—what?"

"She agrees," Argo clarified.

"You can grant us any wish?" Varric asked.

"No. But I am capable of preparing your way." Kimarda keened a sound like a long, low whistle of wind. Her frill flared on her head as she raised her snout upward. Light radiated through the skin of her throat and floated to her lips. Bending forward, she spit a shiny pink pearl onto the rocks at their feet. "Place this pearl in a body of water. For one full day, that water will become a portal to anywhere of your choosing."

Varric grabbed the pearl. It was a little bigger than an Orbeel. He looked from it to Kimarda's throat. "Are you some kind of clam?"

Kimarda's eyes sharpened.

"Ignore him." Setia laughed awkwardly, shooting Varric a hostile glare. "This will take us to Khalkar even though we've never been there?"

"Correct," Kimarda said. "Envision your destination, even if in name only. If such a place exists, the portal will find it. Be aware that the portal closes within one day's time. It cannot be reopened."

"Thanks a lot," Varric said. "We appreciate your help."

"Now leave me." Kimarda rumbled in her throat. "Depart through the pool into which you fell upon your arrival. It will return you to the Forest of Reflections."

"Will that activate the pearl?" Setia asked.

Kimarda squinted at her. "You have a clever mind." She blew on the pearl in Varric's hands, covering it with an extra shiny sheen. When the glow vanished, the pearl sparkled with tiny, shimmering crystals. "I have placed magic over the pearl. It will not activate in water until one night has passed."

"You were trying to trick us?" Varric stuffed the pearl into his belt pouch.

"Consider it another test. And let me warn you, humans. Share nothing you know of this realm or the challenges I impose. I often peek through portals throughout the realms. Should you share of my secrets, I will learn of it. It will not go well for you if you betray me."

"We promise to keep your secrets," Argo assured her. He glanced at the others, leading Varric and Setia to nod. Frodis chirped from his shoulder.

"Then go. Your humanity defiles my domain. Return at your own peril. I will not be gracious to you a second time." Kimarda huffed, flared her neck frill, and sank into her pink pond. The water splashed over the rocks and went still, returning it to its glass-like pink surface.

Varric peeked into the pond and found it was still only a couple of inches deep. She must have created a portal through it.

"Let's not overstay our welcome." Argo set a hand on Varric's back and ushered him away from the Blushing Pond, toward the pool they'd fallen into earlier. He did likewise with Setia.

"Thanks, Kimarda!" Varric shouted over his shoulder.

Varric, Argo, and Setia sat on the edge of the pool of water that would return them to the Forest of Reflections. Cool air moved around Varric's legs, but it wasn't wet. He and the

others shared a look of agreement, and together they slid into
the pool.

Chapter 17

Escape into the Bog

Varric and his allies dropped out of a portal and plummeted into a deep pool of water. Varric popped his head into the air and gasped for breath, flailing to shore in his baggy clothes and heavy cloak. He and the others climbed out of the water and onto the grass. As promised by Kimarda, they found themselves in the Forest of Reflections, but not in the same area as before. Sunset colors streaked through the trees. They hadn't even been gone for a full day.

"Thanks for the help, Frodis," Argo said, patting the Mindling before sending him away.

"Looks like we're on a different side of the forest." Setia twisted her hair, forcing out a significant amount of water.

"Good thing you have an Interloper, huh?" Varric grinned smugly as he twisted water out of his cloak. "Otherwise you might get lost."

Setia shoved his shoulder. "Where did all the Leaflings go?"

"We passed the test. Maybe they'll leave us alone." Argo swept his fingers through his hair, shaking out the wet strands. "Let's head back to Iloria for now. We can gather supplies and rest tonight before heading to Khalkar."

Varric swept his fingers through his hair like Argo, but his hand got stuck in a bunch of snarls. He sheepishly tucked his hands under his cloak. "And get some food, yeah?" he asked.

He was about to teleport when something slammed into him from behind and sent him flying back into the water. As he splashed at the surface, he heard Argo calling his name. Then he sank, and all traces of sunlight vanished in a whirlwind of darkness. Dark creatures dove into the water and surrounded him. They snatched his arms and clothes. In the flurry of bubbles, he recognized the leathery wings and sharp tails of the Wastelings. He couldn't swim with them grabbing him, so he teleported out of the water—bringing a swarm of Wastelings and lots of water with him. The Wastelings piled on top of him so he couldn't get away. If only he had his dagger!

One Wasteling yanked him to his feet, and several others grabbed his arms and cloak, hoisting him off the ground. Dozens of Wastelings swarmed the forest. Varric glimpsed Argo with Novi's wings at his back, slashing his ax and sending countless Wastelings to Radomere. He was fighting his way toward Varric. Setia had out her wings and stabbed Wastelings with her spear. The surrounding pools exploded upward in great fountains. Crablings burst out of the water.

"Cerbrus!" Argo summoned the ice dog as the Crablings leaped at them.

The Wastelings finally got a good grip on Varric and hoisted him into the air. He thrashed his arms and legs and teleported back to the ground. Getting carried away and then accidentally falling wasn't something he wanted to do. He teleported himself and his allies to the sprawling fields between Iloria and Bernadea's house. Of course, he teleported every nearby Wasteling and Crabling with them.

Several portals appeared around them. Wastelings and Crablings by the dozens poured out of them.

"I-impossible," Varric muttered. "How are they following us?"

Wastelings swarmed him again, lifting him off his feet despite his resistance. He teleported him and his allies again, once to the wastes of Clobalt and then back to the far edge of the Forest of Reflections, hoping to shake some of their foes. He staggered from exhaustion from teleporting so many bodies at once. His efforts were fruitful—for a moment. More portals appeared, and an army of foes fell out. When a handful of Wastelings lifted him into the air, he no longer had the energy to resist.

Argo and Setia fought on the ground. When they noticed Varric being carried away, they took to the sky in pursuit. The Crablings gave chase through the forest, bringing down lines of trees. Cerbrus tackled them and ceased their advances. Argo cut through every Wasteling he neared. Setia knocked everything she could out of the air. Yet they fell behind, and Varric filled with dread that they wouldn't reach him.

Then he heard Setia shout, "Enough!"

Storm clouds swirled overhead. Lightning flashed and wind gusted. Rain and hail fell. Varric yelped as a few pea-sized hailstones pelted him, chilling him through his wet clothes. Bolts of lightning shot through Wastelings in every direction. Zapped Wastelings plummeted to the ground while others shrieked and fled into portals. The ones carrying Varric let him go. He cried out as he dropped through violent wind and rain and then splashed into dark, thick sludge. He sat up, completely covered in bog goo.

A Crabling leaped out of a nearby row of trees and clicked its pincers at him. Cerbrus caught it with his fangs and hurled it through the air before it reached Varric. Varric teleported it back to the wastes of Clobalt. A few more ice pellets hit him in the head, but then the storm died to a rainy drizzle and the winds ceased. Clouds parted and gave way to sun. Cerbrus glanced at Varric and then disappeared. All the Wastelings and Crablings had vanished.

"Ugh . . ." Setia murmured from somewhere behind him. "Disgusting."

Varric turned to find Setia and Argo sitting up in the bog, completely covered by nasty black sludge. Not only sludge, but slimy weeds and slugs, too. Even Varric crinkled his nose at the smell.

"I think you need a little more control over that Stormling magic," Argo said as good naturedly as possible since he was sitting in muck, too. Novi and his ax had vanished. "You're not supposed to blow your allies out of the air along with your enemies."

"Sorry," Setia said. "It's tough for me to control, especially when I can't focus."

"You hit me with hail," Varric grumbled, chewing the inside of his lip to hide a smile.

"I'm sorry!" Setia slapped her hands down into the bog in defeat. Then she held out her arms and flinched, shaking sludge off her fingers. "I got rid of the Wastelings, didn't I?"

"I guess that was actually pretty cool." Varric grinned.

When she realized he was teasing, she smiled—and then immediately flinched and wiped her lips, sputtering on bog slime that reached her mouth.

"Stormlings only come out during bad weather, right? It must have been hard to touch one of those." Varric stood with much slurping and gulping from underneath him. The sludge was up to his knees and made it hard to move. When he took a step, his foot slipped out of his boot.

"Not the easiest Ethari to copy powers from," Argo said.

He stood and helped Setia up, and then he helped her trudge through the bog toward Varric. Varric fetched his boot out of the muck and teleported himself and his companions to the edge of the bog, where they flopped to the ground. They stared up at clear skies fading to orange. Crickets and bugs resumed chirping after getting quiet during the attack. A few frogs croaked angrily at having their bog invaded.

"What was that about, anyway?" Varric muttered, wiping sludge off his face. He pulled on his boot and winced at the slime that seeped between his toes. "How did they follow us like that?"

2 KING OF REALMS

"Maybe Kimarda sent them? Another test?" Setia started to wring out her hair and gave up immediately. She wiped whatever sludge she could off her skin and clothes, not that it did any good. She looked like she'd rolled in a puddle of mud.

"Somehow I doubt that. If Kimarda wanted to sacrifice us, she could have teleported us to the wastes of Clobalt instead." Argo shook off some black slime. "Those things looked like they were waiting for us."

"I don't like how they followed us when we teleported." Setia folded her arms across her abdomen. "This was definitely intentional."

"But why? Why chase us?" Varric asked.

"We're the only ones interested in getting the relic back. It makes sense they'd want to stop us before we stop them." Setia shrugged and wiped her face again. Sludge dripped from her hair. "Ugh. Let's go back to Iloria. I can't stand this smell."

"Everyone hates an Interloper until he gets you to your bath faster," Varric said in a sing-song fashion, grinning.

She shoved him, which resulted in sludge sliding off his lip and into his mouth. He spit out the bitter taste. It was worse than any food he'd ever eaten—even food out of the garbage.

Even though his head hurt from using so much magic, Varric teleported them to outside Iloria City's gate. He wobbled as they entered, dizzy and chilled. His stomach rumbled angrily. They slopped and slurped into the city and earned a lot of looks. And a lot of crinkled noses. And a lot of people taking wide routes around them. One market stall owner even gagged as they passed, pulling down a curtain to cover his wares and close up his shop.

"How can you stand this all the time?" Setia muttered to Varric. She bowed her head and shielded her face with her hands whenever people passed.

"I don't normally walk around smelling like a bog," Varric stated. Argo raised an eyebrow at him. His cheeks burned. "I don't!"

"Lend me your cloak." Setia covered her face with both hands as they passed several guards who stared intensely at her.

"It's mine."

"Please just lend it to me. I can't handle this."

"Girls," Varric grumbled under his breath. He gave her the cloak even though taking it off made him significantly colder. He regretted giving it to her until she bundled up and sighed in relief.

"Now will you come to the castle?" she asked.

"Nope."

"Why not? We can have hot baths, ample food, and comfortable beds."

Varric wagged his explosive bracelet at her.

"Fine." Setia stomped both feet on the street and faced them, her glare barely peeking out from under her hood. She set her hands on her hips as she focused a harsh look on Argo. "I didn't want to have to do this, but I have no choice. By royal authority, I order you to make him take a bath."

"You order me?" Argo echoed, laughter in his voice.

"Yes. You're the adult. Do something. I command it."

"You can't do that," Varric said, squinting at her.

"I just did," she declared before returning her attention to Argo. "Use the gold I gave you to buy him new clothes, too. And if either of you smell like bog tomorrow, I'm putting you both in the dungeon." She stomped toward the castle, pausing to flap the end of Varric's cloak at him. "And you're not getting this back. It stinks."

"Hey!" Varric shouted, but she sprinted down the street and disappeared.

"A bath won't kill you," Argo said as he led the way to the inn.

"It might." Varric wrapped his arms around himself, feeling cold and bare without his cloak.

"Tell you what. Have a bath, and I'll treat you to anything you want to eat tonight. Plus desserts."

Varric's stomach rumbled again. That time, Argo heard it, stopped, and raised an eyebrow. Varric squeezed his belly with both arms and scowled.

"Fine," he relented.

"Good." Argo patted him on the head, which resulted in sludge dripping from his hair and down his face. Varric wiped it away and scowled harder as Argo laughed. "Now, let's get you some new clothes."

Chapter 18
Nice Clothes and Nasty Lies

V arric stood in front of a tub of steaming water. He wrapped his arms around himself and shivered, trying to convince himself that getting into the water would warm him up. He still couldn't bring himself to do it. All three tubs in the room were made of fancy stone and full of steaming water. Iloria had hot and cold running water thanks to Orbeels. It was one of the fancy parts of the inn, and Argo had paid quite a bit extra to rent the bathing area. Argo grabbed soaps and towels from shelves in the spacious room.

"It's a bathtub, Varric. It's not going to bite you." Argo tossed the towels onto a stool near the tub. He sniffed the bar of soap. "The soap doesn't even smell like flowers. Isn't that nice?"

He set the soap next to the towel and began taking off all his various accessories, setting them aside in plain sight where thieves could run in and steal them. Varric scratched his head. Maybe he was overreacting. No one had tried to steal anything lately—except him. The water really did look warm, comforting, and way more appealing than lukewarm river water and crusty old soap. Plus, Argo had promised him a feast afterward. He may as well get the bath part over with so he could move on to the good stuff. As he undressed, he tucked his belt and pouches under a low dresser near his tub. It would be hard for anyone to steal his stuff without him seeing it.

"Hiding things from me?" Argo asked.

"No." Varric stuffed his things in a little deeper, just in case. He had Kimarda's pearl, after all.

Argo only smiled and shook his head. Varric slipped his shirt over his head and cringed as half-dried sludge dripped over him. A plume of stink came with it.

"What's that?" Argo asked, tossing his own filthy shirt aside.

"What's what?"

"The mark on your back."

"What mark?" Varric looked over his shoulder and turned half a circle. Of course, he couldn't see his own back. "I don't have a mark."

Argo dug through the supplies at the back of the room and pulled out a hand mirror with a wooden frame. He waved Varric toward a standing mirror in the dressing area. Argo wiped fog off the mirrors before turning Varric's back to the big mirror and handing him the little mirror. Varric adjusted the hand mirror several times to better see his reflection in the larger mirror—and then almost dropped the hand mirror as he gasped.

A jagged black splotch covered a large portion of his skin in his middle and upper back, over his spine and between his shoulder blades. Black vines spread out from a solid black center.

"That's not supposed to be there," Varric said, panic tightening his voice into a pitiful squeak.

"I didn't think so." Argo inspected the mark, his frown deepening. "Does it hurt?"

"No. I didn't know it was there. I don't know how . . ."

Varric stopped. The Wasteling had hit him there with its hooked tail when it stole the relic. He recalled the searing pain he'd felt. It had hit him in that exact spot. The hand mirror slipped from his fingers, and he bobbled it several times before dropping it. Argo caught it before it hit the floor.

"The Wasteling did this," Varric said. Fear coiled around his chest and made it hard to breathe. "It hit me with its tail when it stole the relic during the Tournament. Once it stopped hurting, I completely forgot about it. I didn't think—I didn't know—"

"Calm down." Argo set the mirror on a shelf in the dressing area. "It hasn't killed you, and I take that as a good sign. It's getting late tonight, but we can check in with Bernadea in the morning and see if she knows anything about this."

"Okay . . ." Varric shivered from anxiety and cold. He wrapped his arms around himself a little tighter. Why did things keep getting worse?

"Good." Argo grinned and rubbed Varric's snarled mess of hair before guiding him back toward the tub. "Now get in the water."

Varric sighed and rolled his eyes.

⚜⚜⚜⚜ ⚜⚜⚜⚜

The following morning, Varric had his fill of piping-hot eggs, porridge, and bread fresh from the oven. He and Argo made their way back to the inn so they could leave a message for Setia with the innkeeper before they visited with Bernadea. For the hundredth time, Varric patted the new travel pouch on his belt. It was his favorite part of his new outfit. It was waterproof and bigger than his last pouch, so he could store lots of food for traveling. Argo had also bought him different foods to take with him, including a few breads, jerky, and dried fruit. He also had a second smaller waterproof pouch where he stored Kimarda's pearl.

Varric smoothed the sleeve of his undershirt, appreciating the soft fabric. He was used to the rough texture of his old clothes, which he usually scraped together from stuff he found in the trash. New fabric was something else entirely. And it was so warm! He might not even need a cloak, but he still resented Setia for taking his old one. Extra warmth never hurt, especially when he had to travel to cold places. Along with his undershirt, he had an outer tunic, belt, comfortable pants, and boots that actually fit. They were all in dark, muted shades of brown, green, and blue.

As they approached the inn, Setia came from the opposite direction. As always, she'd cleaned herself up and looked nice and fancy, with her hair in perfect threads, tunic and pants neatly pressed, and armor tidy. In one hand, she carried a bundle of dark fabric.

"Where are you—" She slowed to a stop, her gaze squarely on Varric. She took him in, her eyes traveling up and down. "Wow. Is this the same kid?"

"Good morning to you, too," Varric muttered. His face burned, and he crossed his arms.

"You look so nice." She grabbed some strands of his hair. "You even got a haircut."

"Argo did it." Varric brushed her hand away, his cheeks getting warmer.

Argo had combed his hair until half his hair fell out—and all the snarls along with it. Varric hadn't realized his hair could be so smooth. He'd messed it up a little, because he didn't want it to look too shiny. It fell to chin length with a few wispy waves he hoped made it look less silky.

"You cut his hair with your ax?" Setia gaped at Argo.

"With a knife." Argo drew a small knife from a sheath on his belt before sliding it back into place.

"Even the clothes are nice." Setia walked a small circle around Varric, taking it all in. "Who picked them?"

"I did," Argo said, grinning. "Always did have an eye for fashion."

"Why do you still look like a thug mercenary, then?" Varric asked, which only widened Argo's grin.

Argo had reverted to his original outfit, though cleaned and repaired. It had dark, torn sleeves, and far too many belts and accessories.

"Varric, you clean up so nice. You look like a noble." Setia pinched the fabric of his undershirt sleeve and then sniffed his shoulder. "And you don't even stink."

Varric pushed her away and scowled. His cheeks kept burning hotter. "Joke's on you. I'm going to go roll in a swamp now."

"Please don't," Argo said, setting a fist on one hip. "It took three baths to get you clean."

"Did not!" Varric's cheeks got so hot his head swam. "Only like two and a half . . ." He crossed his arms and sharpened a glare on Setia. "Now if only I had my cloak back."

She rolled her eyes and shook out the bundle of fabric tucked under her arm. It unraveled into the thickest, fanciest cloak Varric had ever seen. Dark brown in color, it had fancy leather stitching on the edges that made it seem like something a noble in disguise would wear. Setia flung it over his head so it draped around his face like a veil. Its ample weight assured Varric it would be warm. He pulled it off his head and squeezed the fabric, pinching it between his fingers. It was thick enough to provide warmth, soft enough to be a comfy blanket, and smooth enough to make little to no noise when he moved. Absolutely perfect.

"For me?" he asked.

"I still have your old one, if you have sentimental feelings toward it. But I figured Argo would convince you to change after that bog incident. No point in covering fresh clothes with a dirty cloak." Setia shrugged.

Varric tossed the cloak around his shoulders and fastened it at his neck with an elaborate clip tucked into the fabric folds. He pulled up the hood and burrowed into the fabric, pulling it tight so he was wrapped in a little cocoon. It was the warmest fabric he'd ever touched. Warm feelings fluttered up from his belly into his chest, and a huge smile spread on his lips. No one had ever given him such a nice gift. He couldn't even remember the last time he'd received a gift at all. He loved it, even if she'd only given it to him so he wouldn't stink anymore.

"It's perfect," he said, beaming at her. "Thank you!"

She blinked at him with wide eyes. Then her face melted into a smile. She adjusted the fabric to show the metal clip.

"And look. This should help if you ever get caught by Wastelings again and they try to strangle you. Just pull the fastener up, and the whole cloak can be tossed off." She pulled on the fastener and showed how easily it could be undone. "This will make it a lot easier than tying it with strings."

"Thanks!"

Varric practiced with the fastener a few times. It came undone easily, but not so easily that it would fall off on its own. It would definitely help if anything tried to dangle him in midair by his cloak. He liked when it was harder for things to strangle him.

"Well, should we go?" Setia folded her hands behind her back. "I'm worried about Khalkar and the relic."

"I don't think they found their way to Khalkar yet," Varric said. "We must be a step ahead of them. Why else would they attack us? I bet they're trying to slow us down."

"Maybe."

"Either way, we need to check in with Bernadea first," Argo said, hooking his thumb toward the exit of the city and leading the way down the street.

"Why?" Setia asked.

"The Wasteling that stole the relic hit Varric with its tail and left a mark on his back. It isn't pretty."

Varric could hear the concern in Argo's voice. Concern showed on Setia's face, too. The warm feelings in his gut intensified. He couldn't remember ever having friends. Were Argo and Setia his friends now? When had that happened?

His steps slowed. Once he got the explosive bracelet off his wrist, he still had to steal the relic for Jonavad. Doing that would mean betraying Argo and Setia. They'd worked hard to retrieve it, and it belonged to Setia. Varric only wanted to use the relic and give it back, but Jonavad insisted on needing it. The warm, fluttery feelings in his stomach turned into cold, hard rocks that made him sick. If he stole the relic, he might save his mom, but Argo and Setia would hate him for it. Varric didn't know why Jonavad wanted it, so there was no way he could explain it to his friends. Jonavad would be furious if he tried, too.

Suddenly, he wanted to give back all the fancy clothes and delicious food. And he wished he'd never had the warm bath and nice haircut. Argo and Setia were good friends, but Varric wasn't. He was a traitor.

"Varric?" Setia called to him.

He jumped, having halted while they walked ahead of him. They'd been talking to him, but he had no idea what they'd said.

"S-sorry." Varric hurried to catch up with them.

"Are you all right?" Argo asked, the concern obvious once again.

Varric's stomach churned. "Yeah," he lied, not feeling all right at all. "Let's hurry to Bernadea's."

Chapter 19

Setia Spills the Beans

V arric dropped them straight into Bernadea's entrance hall. Argo and Setia looked around in confusion.

"Varric," Setia chided in a harsh whisper.

He shrugged, walked over to the door so it opened and closed, and then returned to his friends. They'd teleported straight into the yard before. Why not the house?

"Bernie! Are you here?" he called out.

Something crashed in the next room. Heated muttering followed. Bernadea hopped into the archway between rooms, repeatedly jumping over a rope she spun over and beneath her. Sweat dotted her skin, and one of her hair buns was in disarray.

"You! How did you get in here?"

"Magic?" Varric shrugged and smiled innocently.

"Remind me to beef up my security." Bernadea narrowed her eyes at him. Turning without ever ceasing her rope-jumping exercise, she hopped and skipped to the main room of her house. "What do you want now?"

Varric and the others followed her. Preena thrashed against her crystal as they passed, as usual.

"We're wondering if you can tell us what a mark left by a Wasteling might do," Argo said.

"A mark? What kind of mark?"

"Black. Dark in the center with veins spreading around it."

"Who has such a mark?" Bernadea asked, squinting at each of them in turn without ever ceasing her jumping.

Trying to keep track of her eyes as they bounced up and down was starting to make Varric sick. Finally, she rope-jumped to the table with her tech device, halted, and dropped the rope to the floor. Poking at the buttons, she brought up strings of letters on her panel.

"What is this thing, anyway?" Varric pointed at the panel.

"It's called a screen," she said without slowing her button pressing. "It shows me the information in any connected Orbeels throughout the realms."

"Screen?" Varric pointed at the square of buttons. "What's that?"

"It's a keypad." She glared at him sideways. "The buttons are called keys."

Varric examined the keys she pressed. They had letters on them. He didn't care to ask why.

Bernadea swiped a towel across her sweaty face. "Sorry to disappoint you, but no one has lived long enough to discern what the Wasteling mark actually does."

"It kills them?" Varric's heart stuttered.

"Not precisely. Anyone with a mark is killed by an Ethari shortly after receiving it."

"Maybe that's why Varric keeps getting attacked by Ethari," Setia whispered, leaning close to Varric and Argo.

"How do I get rid of it?" Varric asked Bernadea, clutching his shirt over his chest.

"So it's you, eh?" Bernadea stared at him, dumbfounded. "Not very good at keeping secrets, are you?" She resumed pressing keys, her fingers flying over the keypad. "The only known way to remove the mark is by ending the life of the Ethari who planted it."

"Kill it?" Varric crinkled his nose at the idea. He didn't want to kill something even if it had meant to hurt him.

"Meaning not simply sending it to Radomere," Argo checked.

"Correct." Bernadea grabbed her rope and resumed her jumping routine. She threw in a few fancy arm twists and a little spin before jogging in place with the rope twirling over and under her. She had crazy good moves for an old lady. "You realize my information doesn't come for free, right? You're paying me for all these disturbances?"

"Don't be greedy, Bernadea," Setia muttered.

"A lady's gotta eat," Bernadea replied fiercely. "And I want to eat a lot. Cakes, cookies, crepes . . . You think I do this jumping for fun?"

"It looks fun," Varric said under his breath.

"You'll get paid. I promise." Setia waved away Bernadea and leaned toward Varric and Argo again. "Now we have another reason to find that Wasteling."

"I don't want to kill it," Varric admitted.

Argo patted him on the head. Something menacing lurked behind his eyes, and Varric realized he'd probably do it for him. Varric appreciated it, but it still made him a little sad.

"So . . . to Khalkar?" Setia whispered.

"You found a way to Khalkar?" Bernadea squealed, startling them. She'd somehow rope-hopped behind Setia and leaned close. Her rope was inches from smacking Setia in the head with each twirl.

"Bernadea," Setia snapped.

"You truly are an impressive bunch. How did you do it? Did you find the Blushing Pond?"

"We did," Argo said.

Bernadea continued hopping, but the rope slipped from her hands and pattered to the floor. Eventually, the rest of her stopped moving. "Truly, you did?" Her face lit up and she entwined her fingers under her chin. "Tell me about it. What's it like? How did you find it? Where is it?"

"We took an oath not to tell." Setia set a hand on her hip.

"Break the oath. I don't mind."

"You definitely don't want us to break this oath." Varric laughed nervously, recalling the not-so-thinly-veiled threats of Kimarda. "Trust me."

"I helped you find a mythological location, and you're not even going to tell me about it?"

"For your safety and ours." Argo offered his most charming smile, which immediately unraveled Bernadea's hostile posture and expression. "Tell you what. If Frodis is fine with it, I'll let you pet him later."

"Fine. But only for you and that dumb-perfect smile of yours, big boy." Bernadea side-eyed Argo. "But you'll tell me about Khalkar."

"Anything we can." Setia nodded. "So shall we go?"

Varric nodded, but Argo pressed his lips into a thin line and looked aside.

"What's wrong?" Varric asked.

"I'm not convinced we should go."

"Why not?" Varric scratched his head. "This was the plan all along and the reason we went to the Blushing Pond."

"Khalkar was hidden for a reason," Argo said. "By entering it, we may be inviting others to follow us."

"But we need to retrieve Iloria's relic," Setia countered. "And we can't let the Wasteling open the gate and release the Sage. If they get one Sage, I have a feeling it will be a lot easier for them to get all three and release Arakaros. We can't let that happen."

"We don't even know if the Wasteling found a way into Khalkar." Argo crossed his arms.

"Right. But for all we know, they might already be there looking for the Sage. It's not something we can risk." Setia crossed her arms, too. Since she was a lot shorter than him and had to look up to make eye contact, it probably wasn't intimidating to him.

"Can you look again and see where the Wasteling is?" Argo asked Bernadea, flashing another smile.

"All right. But only because your merry little band is moderately tolerable." Bernadea poked at the keypad, her eyes scanning the screen. "It spent a significant amount of time jumping to and from Clobalt recently. Paid a visit to Iloria yesterday. Currently in an unknown realm. Can't be tracked."

Varric, Setia, and Argo exchanged looks.

"That unknown realm might be Khalkar," Varric pointed out.

"We can't risk it," Setia said. "If the Wasteling finds a way to Khalkar, we need to stop it."

"And if the Wasteling isn't there?" Argo swept his fingers through his hair and exhaled a sharp puff of air.

"I have something that might help with this," Bernadea said. She held out a tiny metal square with a clear Orbeel embedded in it. "Take this with you. It will copy information from any realms you enter. Then I can add the information to Pellios's info-base to be monitored for breaches. Then I could track if the Wasteling goes there."

"That's brilliant!" Setia took the device.

"This isn't something we want in Pellios's info-base," Argo reminded them sternly. "Khalkar shouldn't be known. It's bad enough we know."

"Well . . . I could always use the information for myself. It wouldn't be the first time I used Pellios's tech without their knowing," Bernadea said. Setia raised an eyebrow at her, causing her to unleash a guilty chuckle. "Forget I said anything.

You heard nothing. But it can be done. Then I could monitor Khalkar for you."

"It sounds like a good plan." Setia set a hand on Argo's crossed arms. "We go in, locate the Sage's gate, ensure the Wasteling isn't there, and then monitor it to ensure the Wasteling never enters Khalkar. With Varric, we'd be able to teleport back to Khalkar whenever we needed. We could teleport straight to the gate."

"Teleport?" Bernadea echoed.

Varric's stomach dropped. He was pretty sure his heart stopped, and he couldn't breathe. Setia realized what she'd said and slapped her hands over her mouth. Argo groaned and ran a hand over his face. Bernadea's lips curled, and she fluttered her eyelashes at Varric.

"You wouldn't by chance be an Interloper, would you?" Squealing, she clapped her hands. "Your merry group just gets more and more exciting! You really are a criminal!"

"I'm sorry," Setia whispered to Varric, who was still having a hard time catching his breath.

"I won't tell," Bernadea said to Varric, though she eyed him like he was something she could poke, prod, and study. "Although child Interlopers are unheard of. That makes you extra special."

Varric glared at Setia. He didn't really blame her, even though he kinda blamed her.

"I'm so sorry," she said. "It slipped out."

"Do you hate me?" Varric asked Bernadea.

"Nah. I'm a bit of an outcast myself." Bernadea adjusted her glasses. "Though if you're going to interlope into my house without knocking, make sure you pop into the entrance hall. Some of my exercises shouldn't be witnessed by outsiders. That's your fair warning."

Preena nodded emphatically in agreement. Varric and Setia laughed.

"What do you have to say about all this?" Argo asked Varric, bringing them back to the original subject.

Varric was surprised to be asked for input. He rubbed the bracelet on his wrist, which he obviously wanted off. He still needed Iloria's relic to save his mom. Those things hadn't changed. But more importantly, he thought about the destruction of his realm and the screams of the people as it collapsed. He didn't want that to happen again. He didn't want more people to suffer.

"I think we have to do whatever it takes to keep the Sage from being released. To protect as many people as possible," he said.

"My. How very grown-up of you." Bernadea adjusted her glasses. She grabbed her jumping rope and resumed her exercise routine, skipping and dancing and frolicking in place. "Take the device or leave it. I'll offer my aid if you want it. And I'll keep everything secret. In exchange for whatever mythological details you can share, of course." She punctuated that statement with a slightly evil laugh.

"What if someone follows us through the portal we create?" Argo asked. "It's open for a day."

"I'll teleport it with us," Varric said.

"You can do that?" Setia asked. "Move inanimate things?" She scooted away when Bernadea's flailing rope got a little too close.

"Yeah. I've moved branches and stuff."

Varric scanned the room and found a spare Orbeel sitting on one of Bernadea's counters full of junk. He teleported it above Setia, and it bounced off her head before falling to the floor. He teleported it back to its proper place, grinning innocently as Setia scowled at him.

"See? I'll just bring the whole portal to Khalkar with us," he said.

"Amazing," Bernadea murmured.

Varric's cheeks burned. He ignored her.

"We'll need to test your magic in Khalkar first," Argo said, his brow still furrowed. "We don't want to move the portal into Khalkar only to learn your powers won't take us out."

"That's fine. I'll test it as soon as we arrive."

"So we're agreed? We're going to Khalkar?" Setia asked.

"I suppose we don't have a choice, even if I don't like it." Argo sighed and ran his hand through his hair, stopping in the middle to scratch his head. "Until Iloria's relic is safe, that Sage is a legitimate threat."

"Cool. I know where we can find some nice puddles for our pearl," Varric said.

He smiled and waved at Bernadea before teleporting them to the Forest of Reflections. He approached the nearest pool and saw a memory from earlier in his life—him burrowed in garbage in an alley, trying to stay warm as rain poured down in sheets. He could still remember the cold chill of the water slithering down his spine as it soaked his clothes. He shuddered.

"What do you see?" Argo asked, his expression soft.

"Nothing important." Varric offered the pearl to Setia. "Who wants to do it?"

"You should, since you're used to teleporting," Setia said.

Varric nodded. Holding the pearl, he concentrated on where he wanted to go: Khalkar, close to the Sage's gate, but somewhere safe from harm. He tossed the pearl into the pool, and it landed with a *ploop* and a little splash. Light flashed over the water, and the memory erased and became an ordinary reflection of blue skies peeking through green foliage.

"I guess that's it," he said.

"Everybody ready?" Argo asked. When they nodded, he gripped Varric's shoulder. "Be ready to get us out of there. We have no idea what we're jumping into."

"I'm ready." Varric sat on the edge of the pool. Argo and Setia sat on either side of him.

"Let's get that relic and protect the gate," Setia said with a determined nod.

The three of them slid together into the pool.

Chapter 20
Firelings, Attack!

The portal dumped them onto rock. Black dust plumed around them and went up Varric's nose and down his throat. He and the others broke into a fit of coughing as they inhaled air that smelled like eggs rotting in an alley dump. Varric rubbed his stinging eyes.

Black particles and smoke hung in the air, and the cloud-cloaked sky had a reddish tint, like a place on fire. The sound of crashing rocks carried on the stale air. Varric also heard slow bubbling sounds. Some of the land was smooth and level, but huge rock formations, spikes, hills, and mountains littered the landscape. Everything was made of the same black stone.

"What is this place?" Varric muttered. He loosened his cloak to combat the encroaching heat.

"Somewhere we shouldn't linger." Argo ran his arm across his forehead, wiping away sweat. "Varric, test your powers. If you can leave, bring the entrance portal here."

"Give it a try," Setia said, her voice a little raspy. She coughed a few times, clearing her throat.

Varric teleported to the Forest of Reflections and returned to his friends in Khalkar without trouble. Since it worked fine, he returned to the Forest of Reflections and concentrated on the pool where they'd used Kimarda's pearl. He focused on the ground around the pool and teleported the whole area straight to Khalkar. It fit in the ground perfectly but looked a little odd—a deep pool of water in grass and dirt surrounded by barren black rock.

"Good work. Now let's look around," Argo said. When Setia coughed again, he frowned in concern. "Pay attention to how you're feeling. If you get lightheaded or dizzy, we should leave. The air is polluted and the heat is dangerous."

"I like the heat." Varric grinned, even though it was pretty stuffy.

"What's wrong with you?" Argo grumbled, wiping his forehead again.

They walked in a direction that looked as good as any.

"When I created the portal, I had it put us down somewhere safe, but somewhere close to the Sage's gate." Varric glanced around. Everything looked the same in every direction. "Should we fly up and look around?"

"No," Argo said. "I don't want to draw attention to us."

"What attention?" Setia asked.

"We're surrounded by Ethari. Lots of them."

"How can you tell?" Varric looked around and saw only rocks.

"As a Bonder, I can sense the presence of Ethari," Argo explained.

Varric's heart raced. Were they going to see some new Ethari? Since Ethari weren't fond of him, it made him a little nervous. Argo and Setia set a fast pace, and he jogged to keep up with them through the rocky terrain. They stopped when the ground rumbled, groaning somewhere deep. A patch of land broke and crumbled away. It fell into a blazing yellow and orange river of molten rock that surged beneath the ground. Varric choked on a breath as he realized lava ran directly below them.

More rocks crumbled away. Several balls of fire burst out of the lava and floated in the air. They unraveled into creatures with squat bodies, stumpy arms and legs, and heads shaped like candle flames. They had huge white saucer eyes that took up most of their faces. Their shapes flickered like living fire.

"Firelings!" Varric exclaimed.

Setia punched his shoulder. "Those are Burnlings."

"Burnlings?" Varric rubbed his shoulder, somewhat disappointed. "Did the person who named them even look at them?"

"If you knew what they were best at, you'd understand how they got their name." Argo set a hand on their backs and urged them down the path, his eyes never leaving the lava splashing out of the newly formed holes. "Keep moving—"

The ground beside them collapsed into surging lava that splashed near their feet. More Burnlings floated out of the liquid fire, crackling at them. They didn't have mouths, but

Varric heard laughter. They were mocking them. The entire area began to shake and crumble.

"Run!" Argo pushed Varric and Setia forward.

Rocks heaved upward ahead of them and then dropped into a stream of lava. A burning, raging river separated them from stable ground. Varric teleported them across, only for more rocks to collapse on the fringes of their current area. Lava bubbled onto the ground. A new Ethari climbed out of the molten rock. They had big, round bodies of black stone with veins of lava running through them. Their mouths were huge and they had giant rock fists.

"Those are . . . ?" Varric glanced at Setia.

"No clue. Name away."

"Lavalings," he said. That one was easy. *Rocklings* was already taken.

The Lavalings smashed their fists on the ground. Fissures spread through the whole area, and lava seeped between the cracks. Behind the Lavalings, the top of a low mountain exploded and spewed lava into the air. The spray of yellow-gold liquid drew Varric's attention to something else shining gold in the sky.

"What are those?" he asked, pointing.

Shining birds made entirely of fire swooped toward them.

"Not good." Argo summoned his ax and then called, "Novi!"

The majestic bird Ethari appeared and perched on his back, lending him her wings. Setia took Argo's cue and summoned her spear and wings. Argo shoved Varric to the ground as a rock whistled past that would have whacked him right in his distracted face. He popped upright and whirled around. All the Lavalings were armed with flaming rocks that they hurled at Varric and the others. Meanwhile, the fire birds dove toward them at high speeds and spit fireballs at them.

Varric and his friends took off running, but they'd never escape the bombardment of rocks and flames. He teleported the falling objects and dropped them on the heads of the Lavalings. He also teleported the fire birds and dropped them into nearby hills and mountains. When the birds crashed, they exploded into billowing flames and shattered the rocks to dust.

"Nice!" Argo exclaimed, and Varric couldn't help the flutter of pride in his chest.

The fire birds reformed and continued their pursuit, and more Lavalings broke through the ground ahead of them. Varric teleported himself and his allies over the Lavalings to the next safe patch of land. Behind them, an army of fire birds, Lavalings, and Burnlings pursued them, covering the sky with glaring yellows and oranges.

"Enough of this. Cerbrus!" Argo summoned the ice-rock Ethari. "Get 'em!"

Cerbrus roared. Ice crystals with pointed ends formed around him. With a jerk of his head, he sent the shards whizzing through the air by the dozens. His icy projectiles clipped birds out of the air, snuffed out the flames of Burnlings, and shattered the rocks of Lavalings. A few Ethari bypassed his attacks, sending fireballs and lava rocks soaring in their direction. Cerbrus howled and created a shield of ice that shattered all the projectiles. He cleared the sky of enemy attacks, only for portals to form by the dozens. Dozens of Wastelings fell out.

"Wastelings!" Setia shouted, her mouth gaping.

"How are they creating portals into this realm?" Varric couldn't believe it.

"I don't know, but I'm getting tired of this." Setia held out her hand, and lightning flashed off her palm.

Clouds churned in the sky and swirled into a vortex. Lightning snaked through the clouds, lashing Wastelings out of the air. Rain poured down and pelted the creatures. Wind struck Varric and the others, but thankfully they were far enough away that it wasn't bad. The way the Wastelings got blasted around, he was surprised anyone survived Setia's last storm.

As the Wastelings tumbled through the air, they fell into portals and disappeared. Then more portals appeared and more Wastelings flew out. Setia's storm diminished and a flock of Wastelings darted past them toward a pointy hill in the distance. On its peak sat a giant rainbow Orbeel. See-through flames danced around the Orbeel like some kind of mirage.

"That looks very . . . " Varric wasn't sure what else to say. Weird? Out of place?

"Human-made," Setia finished. "Let's go."

Setia sprang into the air with her wings. Argo scooped up Varric on one arm and kept his other arm handy for his ax, taking flight on Novi's wings. Enemy Ethari pursued them, but Cerbrus built walls of ice against them and their attacks.

Several fire birds broke out of the flock and soared over the icy walls, rising high and then diving low. They had Lavalings in their fiery talons.

"Look out!" Varric shouted.

Argo and Setia dove into evasive maneuvers while the fire birds hurled Lavalings at them. Varric teleported the Lavalings and fire birds to the ground, where they crashed and exploded. From his current height, Varric got a good look at the open rocky spaces near the Orbeel hill and teleported closer. Argo and Setia landed, both sweating and panting from using too much magic. Varric ignored his aching head and body.

The Orbeel hill stood on a lower level of ground ringed by churning lava. Only a narrow bridge of stone led to the low-lying area. The hill itself wasn't particularly tall or wide, but the Orbeel on top was imposing. Two enormous doors made of silver and gold were set in the side of the hill, completely at odds with the rest of Khalkar's landscape. That was the Sage's gate? Varric's heart stuttered at the sight of it. The doors were identical to the ones in his home realm that his father had tried to open, resulting in the destruction of his realm.

Leathery flapping wings distracted Varric. Several Wastelings whizzed past their heads. Argo cleaved some into Radomere as they flew past, but others escaped the range of his blade.

"That one has the relic!" Setia shouted, pointing out one of the passing Wastelings.

Sure enough, it carried Iloria's relic with its six bug legs, and it headed straight for the doors.

"No!" Varric teleported the Wasteling away from the door, but his magic didn't work. He took a step back, his heart skipping a beat. "I can't stop it!"

Varric teleported himself and his friends onto the lower level, hoping to stop the Wasteling before it reached the gate. To his horror, Novi vanished, and so did Setia's wings. Cerbrus jumped over the ring of lava to join them, but he disappeared in a flash. Varric's heart dropped to his feet as his magic shriveled up inside him.

"My magic—" Setia ducked as a Wasteling hurled past her head. It was the one with Iloria's relic. "Varric, stop it!"

"My magic is blocked, too," Varric said in despair.

No other Wastelings approached the gate, only the one with the relic. Varric and the others chased it, desperate to stop it. The ground shuddered beneath them. Several pairs of jointed legs wrapped around the side of the rocky hill. The legs were sharp and slender, like a spider's legs, only giant. Varric, Setia, and Argo slid to a stop as the legs scuttled around the hill, revealing the top of a monstrous shape on the other side, partially blurred by smoke. The Wasteling flapped urgently toward the gate, unconcerned.

An appendage shot around the hill so quickly Varric barely saw it coming. In one thrust, a sword-blade tail stabbed the Wasteling out of the air and skewered it.

Chapter 21

Guardian of the Gate

S kewered, the Wasteling's body went rigid. Its legs splayed outward and the relic clattered to the ground. A jolt of pain cut through Varric's back, followed by a cold sensation that washed over his skin and through his chest. He stumbled and gasped.

"Varric, are you okay?" Argo asked.

"I think the mark disappeared."

Varric realized what that meant. Even though the Wasteling had caused them trouble, he still felt bad it had died.

He and the others sprinted toward the relic. The ground rumbled and the rocky hill shuddered as the mystery monster crawled around and revealed itself. Shaped similar to a spider, it had eight legs, a bulbous body, and a shining rainbow Orbeel the size of an apple on its head. Its huge eyes looked like thousands of glass lenses with fire blazing inside them. Veins of lava ran across its body. Out of its backside stuck a scorpion's tail with a sword-like point. It flicked the skewered Wasteling into the lava.

The spider leaped off its perch and spit plumes of fire in front of the gate, forcing Varric and the others back. The monster crashed in front of them, legs splayed around the relic. Then it stabbed its tail under the relic's handle and flipped the object into the air. In one swift motion, it swallowed the relic whole.

"Did it just—" Varric choked on his words.

"Yup." Argo slid one foot forward, both hands gripping his ax handle.

"My family's relic!" Setia stomped forward, ready for a fight, but the creature screeched and spit out huge fireballs at them.

They dove in different directions, dodging the flames. The fireballs slammed into an invisible wall behind them.

"Oh no." Varric ran to the rock bridge leading to the upper level and slammed into the invisible wall. He pressed against it, but it felt as solid as rock. Light flickered under his palms. "We're trapped!"

On the ledge above, countless Ethari gathered and watched. The Wastelings and Burnlings crackled with sounds of laughter.

"What do we do?" Varric pressed his back to the invisible wall. The only time he'd ever felt more trapped and helpless was when his realm had collapsed around him.

"We have to get the relic," Setia shouted, scowling at the beast. "By any means necessary."

The spider leaped to flatten them. Varric, Argo, and Setia dove out of the way and fled to the area near the doors. They had a lot of space, but against a thing that could jump, stab, and spit fire, they didn't stand a chance without magic.

"Is this thing an Ethari?" Setia asked, rasping and coughing from the fumes.

"No. I sense nothing from it. And look at its head," Argo said.

"The Orbeel?" Varric asked.

"This thing is powered by magic. It's not alive. Steal or break the Orbeel on its head, and I bet the beast falls apart," Argo said.

Stabby spider wasn't about to let them steal or break anything. It shrieked a sound like a knife scraping across rock, which was so piercing it stabbed through Varric's ears and left them ringing. Setia covered her ears, and Argo winced. The beast unhinged its jaws and unleashed waves of flames at them. Varric hit the ground and rolled, covering himself with his cloak as fire swept over him. He felt the heat on his back. Immediately after the flames passed, he rolled across the ground to extinguish the fire on his cloak. Argo and Setia rose, both smoky but okay.

"Setia, distract this thing. I'm going after its Orbeel," Argo commanded, and Setia nodded.

"What about me?" Varric asked.

"Stay as far away from it as possible."

Argo marched a slow circle around the beast, but it followed him with its eyes. Setia stabbed its front leg and drew its

attention long enough for Argo to make a leap for its back.
The creature was too large and smart. It flicked out its leg
and tripped Setia and then heaved sideways to slam Argo with
its body. Varric flinched as his friends hit the ground and the
spider summoned another throat full of flames.

"Fire! Look out," he shouted at them.

Flames curled over and around them, but they both rolled
aside before the wave hit. When the fire cleared, Setia slammed
her spear into the underside of the creature's head. It thrashed
its whole body and knocked her down. Then it reared on its
back legs, clawed the air, and fell over her.

"Setia!" Varric bolted into its back legs, tackling them out
from underneath it.

The beast flopped onto its side, barely missing Setia. Argo
leaped on it from the other direction. He sliced his ax blade
toward the beast's Orbeel. The spider jerked to the side and
knocked off his aim. Its stabby tail shot forward. Argo heaved
his ax sideways and deflected the blade, but the side of the tail
clipped him and hurled him into the air. He hit the hill above
the Sage's gate and tumbled into a cleft of rocks.

Varric and Setia regrouped as the spider stood. It hissed and
spit lava, stamping its legs like it was throwing the world's
ugliest temper tantrum. Argo stood on a rock ledge on the
hill and gestured at them and the spider. Then he gestured at
himself and the giant Orbeel at the hill's peak. With his ax still
in hand, he climbed at a rapid pace.

"Why?" Varric asked, not understanding. He pressed to
Setia's side for a bit of extra courage.

"I don't . . ." Setia shook her head, and then realization dawned in her eyes. "Orbeels provide magical power." She bumped against the invisible wall behind them. "That big Orbeel on the hill might be what's trapping us and sealing our magic. If he can break it, we might get our magic back. Then we can deal with the Orbeel on that thing's head."

"I sure hope so. Here it comes!"

Varric shoved Setia aside and ducked as the sharp-edged tail hit the wall where they'd been standing and skittered off in a shower of sparks. He dove one way and Setia the other way. The spider followed him, gnashing its fangs at him. It spit dozens of fireballs. Varric bolted around the perimeter of the invisible wall, outrunning them. After running a circle and nearing Setia, he reversed, kicked off the invisible wall, and leaped over the fireballs. The spider chased Setia next, shooting fireballs at her. At least she was faster than Varric.

A flash of light from the top of the hill ceased the spider's attack and drew its gaze. Argo slammed his ax blade into the giant Orbeel on the hill. Every blow emitted a flash of light and a loud clang. Glowing cracks spread through its surface.

The spider scuttled onto the rocks after Argo. Varric and Setia ran to stop it. If it didn't want the Orbeel broken, then they did. Varric caught its tail and sank to the ground with it. With her spear, Setia repeatedly stabbed the tail at a joint. The appendage snapped off, drawing a vicious roar from the creature. It whipped around and spewed flames over them, forcing them back.

The giant Orbeel shattered. A gust of wind hurled down the hill and blew the spider to the ground. Varric and Setia lunged aside to avoid being crushed as it tumbled. Boulders rolled off the rock hill, and the whole area shook. The invisible wall flashed and disappeared. Varric's magic flooded back into him. He immediately tried to teleport the spider's Orbeel into his hand, but it didn't work. If he had a weapon, he could teleport onto its head and—

The spider screamed and stomped on the ground with all eight legs. A pulse of magic shot out from it like a gust of strong wind combined with an earthquake. Rocks and lava heaved upward around it. Varric teleported to the upper ledge, then looked back. In the heaving rocks, he saw Setia tossed into the air like a ragdoll—unconscious, or worse. Varric choked for air. The spider moved beneath her and opened its mouth, but Varric teleported her to the edge of Iloria City. He hoped she would wake up and get help for herself, or that someone would find her and help her.

He shook aside those thoughts as the spider turned and set its fractured eyes on Argo, who had fallen off the hill in the upheaval. Argo slowly got to one knee like he was in a lot of pain. His ax lay several feet away from him. Summoning the weapon into his bracer, he pressed his back to the Sage's gate and rose to his feet. The spider cornered him there. Varric chewed his lip. Argo had already used a lot of magic and probably didn't have much strength left. Varric could send him to help Setia—to help them both and protect them from the spider while Varric figured things out. It would be easier with friends, but he couldn't let them die.

The spider leaped at Argo with fangs bared. Varric met Argo's eyes and must have worn his intentions plain on his face.

"Varric, don't—" Argo shouted, but Varric teleported him to Iloria with Setia.

The spider smashed into the doors and then turned, its sharp legs clacking on the rocks. A chorus of crackles and hisses arose behind Varric, and lights flashed in the corners of his eyes. He whirled around to find an army of fire birds, Burnlings, Lavalings, and Wastelings closing in on him. Stabby spider leaped at him from the other side. Flames dropped over him from all directions.

Varric teleported in front of the doors as the spider landed in a whirlwind of flames. All the creatures pursued him to the lower level. He had to do something to stop them, break the Orbeel, and get the relic. For his mom and sisters. For Setia and Argo. A glint of silver drew his attention to the rocks near the door. Setia had dropped her spear. He teleported it into his hand as the spider launched flames at him and fire birds dove at him. Burnlings shot fireballs and Lavalings hurled balls of lava at him, while Wastelings cackled and flocked nearby, ready to strike after the flames roasted him.

Varric needed to put out some fires. He concentrated on the countless ponds in the Forest of Reflections. Summoning all that water to Khalkar, he dropped it in one huge wave over his attackers. The flames of the fire birds extinguished, leaving behind bodies that looked like featherless chickens. They scuttled away on their talons, their nubbin wings useless for flight. The Burnlings melted into tiny flickering flames, and the Lavalings sizzled and shriveled into charred husks. Both fled into the lava. The deluge slammed the Wastelings to the ground. Portals appeared around them, allowing them to flee. Varric didn't bother stopping them.

He focused on the Orbeel on the spider. His water wave had knocked the creature off its feet. It stood in a rush, its body smashing against several spikes of stone that jutted out of the ground behind it. They were surrounded by spikes, and that gave Varric an idea.

Focusing on as many spikes as he could, he teleported them over the unsuspecting spider and let them fall. Spikes slammed through its body and bashed into its head. The creature roared and flailed at the onslaught, thrashing its legs, breaking countless rocks, and hurling them back in pieces at Varric. Varric created a portal in front of him to use as a shield. The rock pieces flew through the portal and reappeared in the distance behind him. It almost worked perfectly, but some fairly large rocks flew over the top of the portal and clipped him on the head.

He hit the ground hard on his back, the air rushing from his lungs. Pain and exhaustion tore through his body. Still, he got to his hands and knees and looked at the beast. It didn't move. Several rock spikes skewered it to the ground. Varric scrambled over to it and shoved the tip of the spear under the Orbeel in its head to pry it out. It wouldn't budge. He wiggled the spear and pushed his magic into it, willing the Orbeel to teleport out of the spider and into the air. A flash of light swept over it, and the rainbow Orbeel popped out and clattered to the ground. Varric hopped after it. The spider beast dissolved and disappeared, and the relic hit the rocks.

Varric held still, catching his breath and anticipating something else leaping out at him. It was quiet. After all the crashing and shrieking, he barely registered the sounds of rocks cracking and lava splashing around him. His legs wobbled. His lungs constricted. He scanned the area and did a double take. Near a cluster of rocks, through billowing smoke and ash, he thought he glimpsed a person wearing a cloak and hood—and he thought he saw some white hair, too. He rubbed his sore eyes and squinted. Then he saw only rocks and smoke.

Knoll? There was no way he could have reached Khalkar. Unless . . . No. Varric shook his head. Interlopers were rare. It had to be his imagination.

Nearby shrieks cut through his thoughts. More Ethari popped out of hiding, their flames reignited. Varric grabbed the relic and Orbeel and teleported out of Khalkar.

Chapter 22

The Relic's Magic

V arric plopped down in lush grass and weeds, his arms wrapped securely around the relic, the Orbeel, and Setia's spear. It felt weird lying on soft ground after rolling around on the hard rocks in Khalkar. Tall trees rustled over his head and covered him in shadows. The dim lighting came as a relief to his throbbing head and itchy eyes. He took a breath and immediately started coughing and wheezing as the fresh air hit his ash-filled lungs.

"Varric?" Argo's voice arose from a slight distance.

Rolling over, Varric climbed to his feet as Argo and Setia ran from Iloria City's gate to meet him in the shadows. Argo reached him first and grabbed his shoulders, relief flooding his eyes. He wrapped Varric in his big arms and squeezed. Varric flinched from the pressure on his sore muscles, but he smiled anyway. A hug was nice for a change.

"Don't you ever do that again," Argo said, holding Varric back and looking him over. "Are you hurt?"

"I'm okay." Varric held up the things he'd brought back. "Look! I got it!"

"Yes. Because that's what we've been worried about." Setia rolled her eyes and wrapped an arm around Varric. He was glad she seemed perfectly fine. Echoing his sentiments, she said, "I'm glad you're safe."

When she released him, Varric glanced around the area. He'd expected Wastelings to chase him since they kept following him around, especially with all the portals popping up in Khalkar.

"Nothing chased us this time," he said. "I thought the Wastelings would follow me here."

"Is that the Orbeel from the creature's head?" Argo pointed at the item in Varric's hand.

"Yeah. I stabbed it out." Varric handed Setia her spear.

"Thanks." She returned it to her bracer, then asked, "You beat that creature by yourself? How?"

"Er . . ." Varric rubbed the back of his neck, recalling how she'd said the Forest of Reflections was a special place for the people of Iloria. It would rain and fill the pools again eventually, right? "Don't go to the Forest of Reflections anytime soon, okay?"

Argo and Setia exchanged glances. Setia glared at Varric, but before she could say anything, he handed her the relic.

"This is yours, yeah?"

"What a relief." A huge smile brightened her face. "Now we can get it locked away again and put all this business about the Sages and Arakaros behind us. But first . . ." She turned the item over in her hands, and her smile vanished. "They used it."

"The Wastelings?" Varric frowned.

"Only humans should be able to use Orbeels," Setia said. Ominous shadows covered her eyes.

Varric recalled the cloaked figure. Maybe he hadn't been imagining things after all.

"I thought I saw someone watching me fight for the relic," he admitted. "I didn't get a good look, and then they disappeared."

"That's a troubling thought." Argo crossed his arms.

"I think . . . I think it was Knoll. I think he's an Interloper," Varric said.

"Are you sure?" Setia asked.

"No," Varric admitted. "But the Wastelings teleported all the time. And how else would Knoll leave the wastes?"

"That would explain one use of the relic." Argo rubbed his jaw, his eyes narrowing on the object in Setia's hands. "If he asked it to show him Khalkar, he could teleport there and bring the Wastelings with him."

Varric clenched his fists. Yes, even a magical peek into another realm would give an Interloper access to Khalkar.

"That doesn't explain how he was following us everywhere," Setia said.

"Unless he had a spy." Varric shrugged. He'd seen a Wasteling watching them in Clobalt.

"What? A Wasteling?" Setia shook her head in disbelief. "It's not useful if you don't know what your spy is saying."

"It looked like he did understand the Wastelings, though." Argo shifted his jaw from side to side. "When we saw him, it seemed like they were communicating with him."

"How?"

Argo only shrugged. They set their eyes on the relic that opened the gate to the Sage. It was also part of the key to unleashing Arakaros from his prison. Knoll didn't like humans. Did he hate them enough to want to release Arakaros and destroy everyone?

Setia squeezed the relic in both hands. Her frustration and concern melted into sadness and defeat, like someone had taken her dessert and thrown it on the floor. And stepped on it. And kicked it into some mud.

"What's wrong?" Argo asked.

"I promised you both an opportunity to use it." Setia turned the relic, showing the three Orbeels Varric had noticed when he'd tried to steal it. Only one of the Orbeels glowed. The other two had dulled. "Only one Orbeel is shining. Meaning there's only one use left before it's dormant again for one hundred years. I'm so sorry."

Varric glanced at Argo, who returned the look. Varric's overheated body went cold. Ice flowed through his veins all the way to his heart. That might be his only chance to help his mom. Her life was at stake! He needed—

"Let Varric use it," Argo said, startling Varric and Setia. They stared at him, baffled.

"What?" Varric squeaked.

Argo smiled with warmth and affection that Varric didn't think he'd ever seen before—not with his mom, not with anyone, at least not that he could remember.

"Find a way to save your mom, kiddo. You're the one who earned it."

Setia nodded and handed Varric the relic. Suddenly, it felt a hundred times heavier than it had before. It held on it the weight of Argo's unfulfilled wish. In getting what he wanted, Varric took Argo's wish from him. Varric gripped the handles and stared at the relic's flat surface. His reflection stared back at him.

"O-okay," he murmured, not believing he had the chance. Not believing someone was kind enough to give it to him. But he kept staring. He couldn't get the words out, and he didn't know why.

"We'll give you a minute." Argo ushered Setia away, apparently assuming Varric's silence was embarrassment or secrecy. They stepped out of hearing range.

Varric stared at them. Argo was giving up his one chance at finding his son so Varric could save his mom. It made Varric's chest ache. He couldn't think of anyone doing anything like that for him before. He'd never had friends before, not really. Not that he could remember.

Jonavad had told him the relic's magic wouldn't save his mom. He'd told him not to bother. Would Varric be wasting the last use of the relic on something doomed to fail when it might successfully find Argo's son instead? Jonavad seemed to think the relic itself would save his mom. Even without using its magic, there might still be a way.

Varric glanced at his friends in the shadows of the trees. Both were covered in soot, proof of their excursion into Khalkar, proof of their struggles together to protect the realms. Varric smiled. The decision became a little easier. He gripped the handles of the relic and looked into its reflective surface.

"Relic, show Argo's son."

The mirror surface of the relic turned black. Then it turned back into a mirror-like reflection with a smoky haze billowing over it. Varric's reflection stared back at him. He frowned and shook the relic. When only his reflection remained on the surface, his stomach sank. It wasn't showing him anything. What did that mean? The surface of the relic turned black again and then returned to its normal, haze-free appearance. The last shining Orbeel blinked out.

Varric's heart sank. He hadn't seen anything. Did it fail to work? Had the Wasteling ruined it? Was it broken? Or did it mean that the thing Varric was looking for didn't exist anymore? Did that mean Argo's son was dead? How could he tell him that? Varric suddenly felt sick. Tears prickled his eyes, but he blinked them away.

"Varric?" Setia called out.

"It . . . it didn't work." Varric returned to them and handed Setia the device. His head and shoulders sagged. No matter how hard he tried, he couldn't look at Argo.

"What do you mean?" Setia checked the dulled Orbeel.

"It went dark, but then it only showed my reflection anyway. Like it didn't have anything to show me." Varric scratched his arm. "Is it broken?" He hoped it was broken. He hoped Argo's son wasn't dead.

"I don't know. It's only used once a century, so we don't know much about it." Setia turned it over in her hands. "I've been told that if it has nothing to show you, it simply won't work. It won't use the Orbeel's power."

"Sorry, kid." Argo set a hand on Varric's shoulder, patting affectionately, which only made Varric feel worse. Argo lightly gripped Varric's forearm and turned it to reveal the explosive on his wrist. "We should get this taken care of."

"If you feel comfortable, share whatever details about your mother and your son," Setia said. "I'll use all my resources to help you. After all, you helped bring the relic back to my realm."

Varric was glad at least one of them was happy. He held up the Orbeel from the spider monster. "What should we do with this?"

"It's probably powerful," Argo said. "That beast was made of tough magic. I've never seen anything like it."

"Let's take it to Bernadea and see if she knows anything about it." Setia pulled out the device with the clear Orbeel that Bernadea had given them. "I want to give her this, too, before we return to the city." Setia glanced at the nearby gate. "I don't want it to fall into anyone else's hands. Especially not people who may have access to the relic."

"You don't trust your father?" Varric asked.

"People other than my father have access to it. I'd hate for them to have access to Khalkar, too. I don't want to take any chances." Setia tucked the device away and wrapped the relic in both arms like she expected a Wasteling to swoop down and steal it.

"That's fair." Argo crossed his arms. "Let's see if Bernadea will monitor Khalkar for a while, too. Just to make sure there's no shady business happening there. Especially if Varric saw another human there."

"Maybe." Varric shrugged.

Maybe it was because he was tired, hungry, and a little sick to his stomach, but he felt rattled. He'd lost an opportunity to find a way to save his mom. Argo's son might be dead. Even though they'd retrieved the relic and he'd get the explosive removed, he still had to find a way to steal the relic later so he could bring it to Jonavad. But they had protected the realms from the Sage, so it wasn't a complete loss. His heart hurt anyway.

"You did good, kid. Even if it didn't turn out the way you wanted." Argo wrapped an arm around Varric's shoulders, which only made him feel worse.

"Yeah . . ."

"Let's go." Setia patted Varric's shoulder. "You must be exhausted after fighting that spider."

Varric nodded. "Yeah. And it was tough moving all those ponds."

"Ponds?" Setia stopped. "You said something earlier about the Forest of Reflections . . ."

"Um, we better hurry before the Wastelings catch up with us." Varric bit his lip and teleported them to Bernadea's before Setia had time to react.

Chapter 23

Freedom Comes with Bounty Hunters

I loria's throne room was as vast and foreboding as Varric remembered it. He and Argo followed Setia inside, approaching the throne. It was the first time Varric noticed that a waterfall covered most of the back wall, framing the throne. The same crowd gathered in the room as before, including nobles in fancy clothes and guards in leather armor. The king, Garthro, sat on his seat on the dais that overlooked the hall. A few servant girls stood near the king, including the girl with the golden gown and curled hair. Wark, the man who'd put the explosive on Varric, also stood with the king.

The crowd whispered to each other when Setia first appeared with the relic. They called out some quiet congratulations. Some clapped their hands. Setia had received similar cheers on her way through Iloria City from anyone who recognized the relic. Many people wore awe on their faces to even see the relic. After all, it was a treasure seen only once every one hundred years.

Varric and Argo stopped at a slight distance from the throne as Setia proceeded onto the platform.

"Father." With her head bowed, she set the relic in her father's hands and then retreated to the green carpet.

Garthro inspected the object, his eyes flashing with muted anger as they landed on the dulled Orbeels. Others in the surrounding audience cheered a little louder. Varric felt a prickle of pride at having accomplished something meaningful. It felt like the first thing he'd ever accomplished in his life. The feeling was hastily crushed by the fact that he'd originally tried to steal it—and would probably have to steal it again.

"Silence," the king said, cutting off all the joyous sounds in the room. Smiling faces and twinkling eyes turned rigid and cold. Garthro's gaze locked on Varric, and soon all eyes in the room followed. "You have done well, Setia," he said, still looking at Varric.

"I didn't do it alone, Father," she said, causing many in the room to shift uncomfortably. Varric squirmed, too.

"You understand the predicament you've put me in, don't you?" The king's glare didn't move from Varric. His eyes narrowed.

"What predicament?" Setia asked. "He fulfilled his end of the deal. Please remove the explosive device and release him."

"How am I supposed to allow an Interloper to go free? You are dangerous. A menace to society," Garthro said.

"I'm sorry for trying to steal the relic," Varric said, the words coming out squeaky. He cleared his throat. "But I'm not dangerous. I don't want to hurt anyone."

"So says the Interloper." The king scoffed, and a few nobles in the audience laughed. So did the attendant girl in her golden gown.

"You said you'd set me free if I brought back the relic."

"So I did. Thus the predicament."

Cold realization washed over Varric and made him shudder. "You never intended to set me free. You hoped I'd die trying to get the relic back. You hoped something else would kill me so you wouldn't feel guilty about killing a kid."

"Father, is that true?" Setia's hands clenched into fists. "You made a deal. Will you go back on your word and make yourself a liar?"

The crowd whispered behind their hands and the king's eyes flashed with quiet rage.

"Silence," he commanded, his voice booming through the hall. Everyone complied. "Wark, remove his bracelet."

"Your Majesty—" Wark started.

"Do it."

Snarling at Varric, Wark strode off the platform. He yanked Varric's arm out from beneath his cloak, squeezing at the elbow. Varric gritted his teeth and refused to give him a reaction. Out of the corner of his eye, he saw Argo straighten and cross his arms, ready to pick a fight if Wark did anything else. Wark touched a metal device against the bracelet. The explosive cuff opened, and Wark took it and returned to his position by the king.

"And my dagger?" Varric rubbed his wrist, which was sore and sensitive after being wrapped up for so long. It was also pretty dirty since he hadn't washed well underneath it in a long time. He pulled his sleeve down to cover it.

Garthro maintained his glare on Varric without wavering. Again, Varric realized his intention: he'd expected Varric to die, so he'd planned on keeping the dagger for himself. Frowning, the king waved his hand. An attendant passed through a curtain of flowering vines at the back of the hall and returned with Varric's dagger. Varric checked the blade to make sure they hadn't done anything shady with it, and then he sheathed it on his hip. The blade felt comfortably heavy and made him feel much more secure.

"I'm afraid I can't allow an Interloper to freely roam my realm," Garthro said, straightening in his seat and looking down his nose at Varric. "You have three days to finish any unresolved business in my realm. After that, I permanently expel you from Iloria." The king's tone hardened. "I know it will be difficult to enforce this ruling, given your abilities. However, many people saw your face. I will issue a decree in three days' time that any who see you within my realm have my authority to annihilate you. By presenting your body before the throne, I will give them a noble title, land, and an exquisite reward of gold."

Varric's stomach dropped and the air whooshed from his lungs. That was an underhanded death sentence!

"Father!" Setia stomped one foot forward, shaking her head in disbelief. "You're going to send bounty hunters after him!"

"You have three days, Interloper," Garthro said without blinking. He passed the relic to Wark. "Be aware that I intend to place the relic in a secure location under constant guard. Any attempts at theft will lead to immediate execution. This is my decree. Now leave my presence. May I never see you again."

Varric had a few choice words for the king, but he chewed them down and swallowed them. He didn't want to make matters worse for himself or for Setia. He'd gotten rid of the explosive and gotten back his dagger. At least he could leave with his life. As much as he hated the thought of bounty hunters chasing him, he knew few would ever see him again.

Still, he shot the king one last glare before he turned to leave, followed closely by Argo and Setia.

"Setia," the king said. "I would like a few more words with you."

Varric made eye contact with her before she returned to the foot of the throne platform. Guards urged Varric and Argo out the throne room doors and down vast halls full of gurgling waterfalls, vibrant plants, and stone walls interwoven with trees.

"You all right?" Argo asked.

"I guess." Varric shrugged. He pulled back his sleeve and showed his bare arm. "At least I got that thing off."

"That arm needs a bath." Argo grinned, and Varric couldn't help but laugh. Argo became somber, his brow furrowed. "Setia is right. Bounty hunters might come after you."

"I'm used to being on the move," Varric said, unconcerned. If bounty hunters wanted to chase him from gutter to gutter, they could.

The guards led them straight out of the castle, down the stone steps, and out the castle gates. As if that didn't make it clear enough, they shut the metal gate behind them with a loud clang. Varric and Argo looked over their shoulders at the closed doors before setting off down the street. Argo led the way toward the inn, and Varric hoped that meant he'd get at least another night or two in a warm bed. He hoped he'd get some tasty food, too.

On the way, Varric noticed many people staring, recognizing them from when they walked through the city with the rescued relic, or maybe recognizing him from his actions during the Tournament. He wasn't just a street urchin anymore. Now he was the Interloper who had retrieved the relic with the princess. Some may have known him as the kid who tried to steal it, too. Some people nodded with mute expressions. Some smiled. Several glared at him with open hostility and covered their wares, knowing he could easily steal from them. More people glared than nodded in approval, making his heart a little heavier.

"What do you plan to do now?" Argo asked when they reached the front of the inn, a long building built into the root systems of several massive trees.

"Same thing I was doing before." Varric shrugged. "I'll keep searching for ways to help my mom."

"I figured." Argo crossed his arms and shifted his weight from one leg to the other. "In that case, I'd like to go with you."

"Why?" Varric blinked in surprise.

"I've hit a dead end on leads to find my son," Argo said. "At this point, I might have better luck hopping around the realms with you. What do you think?"

Varric mimicked Argo and shifted his weight from side to side. Worry churned in his belly. He still had to steal the relic, which would be tough to do with Argo around. Then again, he wondered if Jonavad would still want it. Jonavad wouldn't have known the true purpose of the relic—that it was a key to the Sage's gate, not some all-powerful relic that could heal broken minds and bodies. Varric didn't think the relic could help his mom, and he didn't want to risk stealing it if it was a misunderstanding on Jonavad's part. Before he made any major decisions, he'd talk to Jonavad. In the meantime, Varric would stay with Argo. If Jonavad decided they didn't need the relic anymore, maybe Argo could come up with some new ideas to help Varric's mom. In return, Varric could help Argo find out what happened to his son.

And if Varric was being honest, he didn't want to be alone anymore.

"I'd like traveling with you for a while longer," Varric said, unable to resist a small smile.

"Good." Argo returned the smile, warm and genuine. He glanced at the inn and then jutted his thumb down the street.

"I'm heading to the transport station. I need to head home for a bit. Want to join me?"

"To Yerevir?" Varric asked, and Argo nodded. Excitement overwhelmed his previous worry. He'd never been to Yerevir, and it would be fun to learn more about Argo. But Varric had to report to Jonavad and learn what he wanted him to do next. "Not right now. I think I'll rest here at the inn for a while."

It wasn't the full truth, but Varric did plan on returning to the inn later. Or maybe he'd have to sleep in some roots under a tree somewhere, since he didn't have gold. Argo considered Varric thoughtfully, nodded, and then handed him a leather pouch of jingling coins. Varric's hand sank under the pouch's weight.

"Use this to get some good food and a room for the night," Argo said as he backed away.

Varric looked in the pouch and found an insane amount of gold coins and nuggets. His heart jumped into his throat. "And a room every night for the rest of my life." Varric looked in shock at Argo. "Is this Setia's?"

"It's mine." Argo grinned, still slowly making his way backward. "You'll be here tomorrow? You're not going to run off on me?"

"I'll be here." Varric didn't know where to put his eyes: the pouch of insane amounts of gold or the man who provided it.

"Then I'll meet you here tomorrow. Rest well." Argo turned and strolled down the street.

"B-bye . . ." Varric watched him disappear into the crowd. It took a while for Argo to move out of sight since he was so tall.

Varric peered again into the pouch. He now had a crazy amount of gold in his possession. Stuffing it into his belt pouch, he tied the satchel inside so it wouldn't be easy to steal. Then he secured the belt pouch, too.

It was time for him to return to Jonavad and explain what happened. The inn always seemed to have rooms available, so he wasn't worried about getting one until later. He bought some sugar-berry treats in the shape of animals for his sisters. With his souvenirs tucked safely in his belt pouch, he crept into the shadows between a building and a tree.

His heart raced at the thought of returning home. It had been a while. He knew Jonavad would be disappointed, but he couldn't avoid him forever. Still, sweat formed on his hands, and his stomach churned in discomfort. Taking a deep breath and steeling himself, he teleported to Sowengard.

Chapter 24

Home

Varric arrived in a hallway lit by a flickering Orbeel light. Collapsed stone blocks filled one side of the passage. The pale stones of the walls and floors, once glossy and bright, were now crumbling and caked in grime. Tall windows, once open to beautiful blue skies and rolling fields, were now boarded and curtained.

Dust swirled up around Varric as he knocked lightly on a lone door in the wall.

"Mother?" he whispered.

He heard nothing, so he peeked inside. The room was mostly dark. A gray sheet covered the Orbeel lamp to keep it dim.

Varric tiptoed inside and found his mom in her usual place: sitting in a rocking chair facing the sealed window. Her vacant gray eyes stared into nothingness and her dirty blond hair fell over her shoulder in a messy braid. She wore a nightshirt too big for her slight form and a shawl over her shoulders that dwarfed her in too much fabric. Her fingers twitched and grabbed the air, fumbling like she was knitting. Her lips moved as she muttered under her breath.

"I'm home, Mother," Varric whispered, stepping closer in case she might see him. She hadn't in eight years, though, so he didn't know why he bothered anymore.

"Is that you, Cyrus?" she asked, her voice faint. Her eyes stared past him to the window.

"N-no, Mother." Varric knelt at her feet. He never wanted to startle her, so he tried to look extra small and harmless in her presence. "It's me."

"I warned you not to get involved, Cyrus." She rocked a little harder in her chair. "I warned you to leave those things alone. But you didn't listen to me."

Varric grimaced. Whenever she spoke, she always spoke about his father, which made sense since her last memory was of his father's betrayal that ruined their realm.

"I've been trying to find ways to help you, Mother." Varric loosely gripped her trembling fingers. She was cold, like she was barely alive.

"I told you not to go." She yanked her hand away from him and wrung her fingers together in front of her chest. She rocked faster in her seat. Never did her eyes waver or blink. "I told you it was a bad idea, Cyrus. I told you not to look into those things. I told you." The speed of her words increased. So did her volume.

"Mother, please—"

"Lady Natalina, are you all right?" One of his mother's attendants, Erin, burst through the door. When she saw

Varric, she frowned. "What are you doing here? What happened?"

"Nothing. She just—"

"It's your fault. All of it," Varric's mom said, getting louder and rocking faster.

"Mother!" Lylia and Rhema rushed in behind Erin, panic all over their faces. Varric's throat clenched. He never wanted his little sisters to see their mom like that.

"Lady Natalina, please," Erin consoled her, pressing on the arm of the rocker to slow it.

His mother's face lifted and her eyes focused on Varric—terrifyingly coherent even though he knew she looked right through him.

"I hate you for all you've done. I warned you, Cyrus," she stated.

Varric pressed his back against the boarded window, staring at his mother in shock. He knew she wasn't speaking to him—he knew those words weren't meant for him—but they stung anyway. His mother's eyes glazed over, but it still seemed like she stared straight at him.

"I hate you," she whispered, and then she began muttering incoherently, getting more and more agitated.

"Please rest, Lady Natalina," Erin said. Then she glared at Varric over her shoulder. "You should go."

Heart cracking, Varric retreated from the room and shut the door. He stared at the wall, listening as Erin and his sisters consoled his mother. She remained the same way she'd been for the past eight years. No, she'd gotten frailer and colder. He was running out of time to save her.

After a little while, his sisters exited the room. Rhema's face split into a huge grin when she saw him. Her gray eyes twinkled through a curtain of dirty blond hair that spilled over her head in every direction. She was a miniature but slightly disheveled version of their mom.

"You're back!" Rhema wrapped her arms around him.

He engulfed her in his arms, scooped her up, and spun her around. Pretty soon, she'd be too big for him to lift, which wasn't fair since she was only eight. Her servant dress plumed around her in waves of gray fabric.

"Another failure, I take it?" Lylia crossed her arms and stood at a slight distance.

Like Varric, she had their father's dark hair and eyes. Unlike Varric, she had their father's stocky build and height. At ten years old, she was already as tall as Varric. She wore her hair in a messy bun and had her servant dress tucked into her oversized boots.

"I ran into some trouble." Varric set Rhema on her feet. "I did everything I could."

"Did you bring us anything?" Rhema asked.

"Of course." Varric took out the treats he brought for them. "Candy from Iloria."

"Thank you!" Rhema hugged him and then meandered away, sucking the sugar off the treat.

"Thanks." Lylia took hers, a little less impressed. "Jonavad says there isn't much time left for Mother."

"I know. I'm doing everything I can. I promise."

"It might not be good enough." Her voice wavered. "Can't you help Mother? We're counting on you."

Varric heard the unspoken words: *and you keep letting us down.*

"I'm trying," he said, because he had been for eight years. He'd done everything Jonavad asked of him. Nothing worked.

"You should see Jonavad." Lylia straightened her face, offered him a quick hug, and turned to walk away. She paused, her expression finally softening to the compassionate little sister he knew still existed under her tough exterior. "I'm glad you're safe."

Lylia took Rhema's hand, and they walked down the hall together. Rhema glanced back with her treat dangling from her mouth. She waved at Varric. He smiled and waved back, even though his heart cracked a bit more.

He hated letting them down. They deserved better. Varric wished something would work out for a change so he could heal his mom, take his sisters, and run far away—to a happier place where they didn't need to seal up the windows because the realm outside was dead.

He teleported into the hall outside Jonavad's office. Jonavad stayed in one of the only remaining royal suites. He'd taken residence there after the realm's collapse. Varric's mom and sisters stayed with the attendants in the servants' quarters. Varric no longer had a room. His had been destroyed.

Varric choked down the persistent lump in his throat. His heart pumped hard and chills swept up his spine as he anticipated the disappointment on Jonavad's face. He took a deep breath and knocked.

"It's me," he said.

"Enter."

Varric stepped into the brilliantly lit room. Orbeel lamps shone from silver sconces on several walls. The pearly white stone floors and walls retained their original color and shine. Rugs trimmed in gold covered the floor. The desk, chairs, dressers, bookshelves, and wardrobe were made of glossy dark wood. Two closed doors in the room led to Jonavad's private bedroom and a personal bathroom.

Jonavad stood behind his desk and gazed out the only remaining window with intact glass. Outside, the sun glared down on a flat landscape of endless dust.

"That took you a long time," Jonavad said. He stood with his hands folded behind him, his chest out and his back stiff. He wore a dark blue suit with gold trim and fastenings. His bright blond hair was parted in the middle, not a strand out of place.

"I ran into some complications," Varric said, grimacing at the nervous tremble in his voice.

He explained to Jonavad everything that had happened since he'd tried to steal the relic. He kept some details a secret, though. He didn't want Jonavad to know too much about Argo, Setia, or Bernadea. They felt too special to him. It felt like Jonavad might take them away if he knew about them. Varric didn't understand the feeling.

"You were foolish. You shouldn't have put yourself in a position to be caught." Jonavad slightly turned. He looked Varric over.

"The Ethari were attacking Iloria," Varric said. "I couldn't—"

"Ethari?"

"Beasts." Varric swallowed hard. Talking to Jonavad was nerve-wracking. He always managed to say the wrong things.

Jonavad stared at him, his piercing green eyes cutting through Varric's defenses and making him feel like a little kid.

"You realize the beasts were following you," Jonavad said. When Varric frowned, he continued, "The mark on your back. Wastelings mark their prey so they can follow them. The Wasteling could perceive your location from anywhere. If they were helped by an Interloper as you believe, they could have used the mark on your back to follow you with considerable ease."

"W-what?" Varric stepped back, horrified.

"I wonder if you led them here." Jonavad didn't sound pleased.

"The mark is gone," Varric said, swallowing hard. Argo had checked to make sure.

"Hmm."

Varric rubbed his forehead against an increasing headache. No wonder the Wastelings followed him everywhere. But why? Did they know about the spider guardian in front of the gate? Did they want him and the others to die? Or maybe defeat it so they could open the Sage's gate easier? At least two things were confirmed. Knoll could definitely communicate with the Wastelings to learn where to open portals while tracking Varric, and . . .

"Knoll is an Interloper," he muttered. "He used Iloria's relic to find a way into Khalkar." Which meant he sent the Wastelings into Iloria during the Tournament to steal it in the first place. Knoll orchestrated everything.

Jonavad sat at his desk. Only then did Varric notice the tray of snacks in front of him. Jonavad plucked a few grapes from a large cluster and popped them into his mouth before creating a miniature sandwich of meat, cheese, and crackers.

"Your blundering on this mission may prove useful," Jonavad said.

"How?"

"I told you I don't care about the relic's magic. I want the Sage."

"You want to open the Sage's gate?" Varric squeaked. "It's too dangerous."

"It's the only way to save your mother. Isn't that what you want?" Jonavad tossed the mini sandwich into his mouth and chewed. "We've tried every possible method. Only powerful magic will save your mother now."

"The Sages were sealed because they can really hurt us."

"I am aware." Jonavad popped a few more grapes into his mouth.

"Then why—"

"Why do you question me? Have I led you astray before?" Jonavad asked, his eyebrows knitted together.

Varric's shoulders sank. No, Jonavad was the only one who had never let him down.

"I want to save your mother," Jonavad said. "But to do that, I need you to trust me. Of course, I don't intend to sacrifice any realms in the process." He went to the wardrobe and dug through layers of fabric, pulling out a small wooden box. He set it on the desk and returned to his seat. "Do you want to save your mother?"

"Of course." Varric struggled to swallow. His mind wandered back to the offers of Setia and Argo, who wanted to help him. Maybe they had safer options than releasing the Sage. "Maybe we could ask for outside help. Maybe—"

Jonavad slammed his hands on the desk and rose in a rush. Varric jumped and retreated to the door. His heart hammered in his chest, and his lungs tightened until he couldn't breathe.

"Have you forgotten what happened here?" Jonavad asked with fire in his voice. "Have eight years clouded your memories?"

Varric shook his head. His throat constricted, and he couldn't speak.

"Your father destroyed this realm and killed countless people. You didn't help, either."

Tears burned Varric's eyes. No, he hadn't helped. Not much, anyway. He'd saved some people, but not enough. Not his mom.

"What will people think of you and your sisters? What will people think of your mother when others know what she allowed her husband to do?" Jonavad asked.

He stepped around the desk and moved closer to Varric. Varric's heart thundered in his chest, and he wiped his hands on his cloak to rid them of a cold sweat.

"Do you think all will be forgiven?" Jonavad continued. "Your family destroyed a realm. You will live in shame for the rest of your lives. You will be hated and feared. Your sisters, too. Is that what you want for them?"

Varric shook his head.

"I am doing everything I can to improve conditions for your family," Jonavad said. "Stop making things difficult for me."

"I'm sorry," Varric said, his throat so tight he barely made a sound. "What do you want me to do?"

"Return to Iloria. I want you to steal the relic, go to Khalkar, and retrieve the Sage." Jonavad opened the chest and gave Varric a small, rainbow-tinted crystal from inside. It reminded Varric of Preena's crystal, only smaller. "This crystal is identical to the ones that originally captured the Sages. Trap the Sage, bring it to me, and we'll use its powers to restore your mother."

Varric turned the crystal over in his hand. Doubt wheedled into his mind. Would his mom approve of that? Would she want them to risk the realms to save her? If all the realms would be in danger because Varric released a Sage, he didn't think it was right.

"Did I stutter?" Jonavad asked, dropping into his chair and tossing another grape into his mouth. "Go. We will save your mother. Even if we have to unleash Arakaros and steal his magic to do it."

"Release Arakaros?" Varric choked on his words. "We can't do that."

"You're right. We can't. But *you* can. And you had better prepare yourself to do it if your mother's condition gets worse. If you want to save her, you need to learn how to take risks and make difficult decisions." Jonavad grabbed a writing quill from an inkhorn and started writing on a piece of parchment. Offhandedly he added, "Your hesitation to use your magic already cost her eight years of her life and caused this whole mess in the first place."

With that, Jonavad ignored Varric and acted like he'd ceased to exist. Varric almost wished he *had* ceased to exist. Jonavad was right. His hesitation had cost his mom and his realm everything. He wouldn't let it stop him from saving her now. His magic would help her.

He was the only one who could use the magic of the Sages. If they couldn't save her, Varric was the only one who could release Arakaros. Arakaros would definitely have enough magic to heal her. But Arakaros hated humans and wanted to destroy the human realms. By pursuing the Sages and Arakaros, Varric would put all the realms at risk. The thought filled him with dread. His dumb magic had the potential to ruin so many innocent lives.

Sometimes, Varric really, really hated being the King of Realms.

Acknowledgements

Writing a novel is tough, and I have lots of people to thank for helping me through the process.

Ali and Ben Lewis, thanks for the photoshoot and the sword. You guys have been a huge part of my writing journey from the start, and sometimes, that sword was the only thing that kept me going.

Sai, thank you for the listening ear and the encouraging words whenever I got down in the dumps. Someday, I will commission you for that Frodis tote bag, because I need that to exist.

Jenny Henthorn, thanks for believing in my ability to succeed and for proofreading my final draft with eagle-focused precision. I miss flinging rubber chickens with (and at) you on a daily basis.

Jill Ende, thanks in advance for being my future driver—it's going to happen. And thanks for encouraging me to keep going, for taking me seriously, and for helping with all of the print-related marketing stuff.

Thank you to all of my alpha and beta readers who helped me along the way. Special thanks to Lisa, Prashant, Tim,

Sheryl, and Nicole, who critiqued my manuscript at various stages of development. I also have to give a huge shout-out to all of my early readers who offered advice and cheered me on while I edited the manuscript a billion times. Thanks to Emery, Landon, Hayley, Kylie, Eden, Becca, Lizzy, Rose, Ana, and Rachel. Your feedback helped me tons.

Much thanks to The Bearded Book Editor, Darcy Werkman, for the brilliant editing work. Thanks also to Chrissy Sugiyama for another set of proofreading eyes on the final draft.

Pintado, thank you so much for creating the gorgeous new cover illustration and design for King of Realms. The new style is epic, and it's PERFECT for an adventure-filled fantasy novel. It's exactly what I needed, and I love it so much!

Mark Anthony Avila (Mark 331), you are still my hero for creating my original covers, which I will forever love to pieces. You brought my characters to life, and I'm still in awe. Thank you!

Thank you to everyone who leaves a review and spreads the word about this book—your support helps me survive as an author.

Last—but certainly not least—thanks to YOU. Thanks for reading my book and joining me for the ride. I hope we can go on many more adventures together.

About the Author

Britt lives in the frigid wasteland known as Minnesota. While she hates the cold and snow, she appreciates the nice summers, the lack of lethal creepy crawlies, and the pretty forests and lakes. Outside of writing, she loves reading, high-speed walking, and high-speed walking while reading—yes, that's a thing, and no, she hasn't accidentally walked off a cliff (yet). One of her favorite places is Japan, where she lived for nearly three years and ate far too many sweet potatoes.